The Break-Up Diaries

Vol. 1

Also by Ni-Ni Simone

SHORTIE LIKE MINE

IF I WAS YOUR GIRL

A GIRL LIKE ME

TEENAGE LOVE AFFAIR

UPGRADE U

Published by Dafina Books

The Break-Up Diaries

Vol. 1

Ni-Ni Simone
Kelli London

Dafina KTeen Books
KENSINGTON PUBLISHING CORP.
www.kensingtonbooks.com/KTeen

DAFINA KTEEN BOOKS are published by

Kensington Publishing Corp.
119 West 40th Street
New York, NY 10018

Copyright © 2011 by Kensington Publishing Corporation
"Hot Boyz" copyright © 2011 by Ni-Ni Simone
"The Boy Trap" copyright © 2011 by Kelli London

ISBN-13: 978-0-7582-6316-2
ISBN-10: 0-7582-6316-3

First Printing: May 2011
10 9 8 7 6 5 4 3 2

Printed in the United States of America

CONTENTS

HOT BOYZ

NI-NI SIMONE

1

This is how we do it . . .

—RICK ROSS, "ASTON MARTIN MUSIC"

Hotlanta, USA

"Well, here goes nothin'. . ." eased into the air as Rick Ross's "Aston Martin Music" boomed from my hot-pink '85 Impala with the custom drop top and tags that read DADDY'S GIRL.

I was on a natural high and there was nothing anyone could say that would ruin this moment— the best moment of my life! I'd just been given the keys to the classic car of my dreams. The very car I had pictures of sprawled about my room for the last two years, as I waited patiently for today—the day I turned sixteen.

Instead of having a fly MTV-esque party, my wish when I blew out the candles was that I'd have a custom and kitted-up ride with twenty-eight-inch white-ball tires planted on the pavers of our Alpharetta circular driveway. And I did.

Now, all I needed was for my night to get poppin'. I already had my girls—Keeya, who was also my aunt, and my two besties, Riunite, who we called Ree-Ree, and her sister Martini, all lined up and ready to get it crunked.

I could tell by the look on my mother's face that she wasn't pleased with my birthday gift, but she didn't dare part her lips. Instead, she smiled. Her complaining is why she and my father were separated in the first place.

I wished she would be happy for me though, instead of faking the funk. It's like, I wanted to connect with her, but she was too busy being the district attorney for the city of Atlanta than to be my mother. It was almost a pity that I was her splitting image: skin the color of smooth maple syrup, coils of natural and thick ebony curls that rested against the small of my back, rich chestnut eyes, and deep-plunging dimples.

Honestly, I didn't know I was beautiful until I turned fifteen. Up until then, my life had been mundane, routine, and filled with self-pity. I spent every day feeling awkward. I'd never played with dolls, never jumped rope, hopscotch, or any other ridiculous game. I didn't have time for things like that.

I was too busy wondering why I had my period at nine, why at twelve I filled out a D-cup bra, and why at fourteen my small waist and size-fourteen hips had more dirty old men hollering at me than I could deal with. Needless to say, most of my childhood was spent indoors.

But the day I turned fifteen was when it all changed: My daddy's gift to me was his family. He decided that since all of my mother's relatives lived in Jersey, I should get to know his family better. That's when the clouds opened up and the real me stepped out of my shell.

I had the coolest fifty-seven-year-old nana in the world, who forced the matron out of me! And thanks to my aunt Keeya—who was only a year older than me—I was put down on this thing called "game." I learned that my insecurities were actually attributes. Better known as a milkshake that, when worked correctly, would bring all the right cuties to the yard. And once those cuties came, I suddenly liked being hollered at and being able to pull whatever cat I wanted. And not only lil young dudes my age, but hot boyz, ages eighteen, nineteen, and beyond. And not some creepy, old-man-type ish, but sexy rap-star-esque, six-pack-havin' type. I'm talkin' fine. The kinda fine that you dream about. Sneak out the house and defy your parents to see about. Those dudes.

That's how I ended up with Derrell. He lived in Bankhead a few blocks over from Nana and Keeya. Derrell was supposed to be a trial run, just enough for me to see if I could handle an older man—nineteen. But being with him was like babysitting. He was such a pest that I had his number programmed into my phone under the name Stalker. He was way too sensitive, said yes too much, had the nerve to cry in front of me once—talk about a turn-off—and to top it all off, he threatened to tell my mother how much fun I really had in the hood if I ever left him. But that was a chance I would take, which was why I planned to rock out my birthday with my home girls and not him.

"Thank you *soooo* much, Daddy!" I gave my father the biggest hug that I could. My arms barely wrapped around his athletic frame, but I did my best to squeeze him.

"Deedra," my father said as he smiled at my mother and pointed to my ride. "You like? Check out the soft pink drop top. It's a nice contrast to the car's color. Peep the chrome rims, and the white leather seats with pink piping trim."

She shot him a struggling grin. "Well, Kaareem, I would've liked a Mercedes better, perhaps a Lexus, but moreover I would've appreciated had you spoken to me first, before you bought *our daughter* a car."

He walked over to her and placed her hands between his. "You're right," he said, a little too much like he cared, which caused my mother to tense up. She didn't do public displays of affection and she especially didn't do them coming from my father. She eased her hands back to her sides.

"Don't try and pacify me," she said, pissed. "We've had this discussion before and every time you do the same thing."

"Can't you be happy for once?" he snapped.

My mother's lips grew stiff. "I'm tired of Chance's presumed unhappiness being the running theme around here. My problem with you, aside from you not understanding the role of a family man, is that Chance, *our child*, just passed her road test this morning and already this evening she has a car. That's a little baffling to me, considering she hasn't done anything to earn it! And I think she would've appreciated having a nice dinner with you a lot more."

I can't believe she said that.

Daddy's chiseled jaw clinched and he shot my mother a nasty eye. He walked over to me and kissed me on my forehead. "Anything for my baby girl." And I knew he meant that. He was the CEO of United Banking Express Inc., a Fortune 500 company, which landed him in *Forbes* twice, so money was never an issue and anything he could buy me I had in the blink of an eye. My mother was pretty much the same way. The only difference was that Daddy always claimed he wanted to spend time with me, while my mother always said, "I have to work to take care of you." Needless to say they were both pretty much always M.I.A.—except for my birthdays and Christmases . . . and maybe an Easter or two—so my mother's tongue-lashing at my father was definitely the pot pissing on the kettle.

But, whatever, their limited time for me didn't bother me anymore. I had a life and I did my own thing. Besides, one thing's for sure and two things for certain with parents like mine, I may not have been legally grown, per se, but I was grown. Trust.

"What do you have planned for your birthday, baby girl?" Daddy asked me, as he turned away from my mother.

My mother stepped to the side of him and interjected, "Whatever it is, it needs to happen before ten-thirty tonight."

I whipped my head quickly toward her. It was already nine o'clock and I really should've been out of here an hour ago. "Since when do I have a curfew in the summer?"

"You have always had a curfew," she said sternly.

"Ma, stop buggin'."

"Stop what?"

"Watch your tone, Chance," my daddy warned.

Ugg! I swear he sided with her at the wrong time. "Ma." I softened my voice and steadied my tone. "Please. You told me I could spend the weekend with Nana and Keeya. And it's my birthday. My sweet sixteen."

"I know what day it is," she said. "I gave birth to you. And it may not have been a car, but I did give you a pair of rare, princess-cut, chocolate diamond earrings. But I don't see you ready to break free and show those off."

"Ma—"

"And," she continued, "I don't think you are responsible enough to drive a car around here like you're grown. Because you are not an adult."

"Ma—"

"And let me tell you something, you got one time to mess up. One time to not come home on a Sunday night and it will be a problem."

She was trippin'. "Ma, it's not that serious."

"Well then, don't go. Stay home." *Is she for real? Does she understand that I just turned sixteen and not six? Clearly there is a difference.* "Ma," I whined, "it's my birthday and I want to go and hang with Keeya—"

"Go hang with Keeya *where*?" she pressed.

"Umm . . . the movies. Nana made a cake for me, so after the movies, we'll be inside celebrating for the rest of the night. I promise."

"Your nana baked a cake? Since when did Mama start cooking?" My father arched his brow. "She's never cooked."

I wish he would shut up.

"Ma—" I whined.

"So what you're telling me is that you want to spend your birthday transforming to ghetto—"

"Ma—"

"And you want to hang—or should I say chill— in the projects watching the crackheads go by? Really? And I should consent to my only child doing that?"

"Ma, I'm not trying to be ghetto and Nana doesn't live in the projects," I said defensively.

"She and most of her neighbors own their homes. They can't help it if it's a crime-riddled housing project down the street. The mayor, city council, and rich investors have intentionally not done anything about that. You told me if the city wanted to really clean that up, they'd decide those changes at a political round table. Now how can you blame Nana for that? She doesn't even like politics."

I could tell my father was impressed. My mother was pissed that I threw her own words back in her face, but hmph, I had to prove my point. The last thing I needed was her placing a wedge between me and my destiny for tonight: McDaniel's Bowling Alley. And no, my plan wasn't to bowl. It was to profile in the parking lot.

"And," I continued, "you really don't have to live in Bankhead to be a crackhead. The actress down the street is a straight fiend and this is a multimillion-dollar gated community."

"Whoa, I'm impressed." She twisted her lips. "Let's see if you can retain that much during the school year. Now, as I said, I would like you to stay home."

"Yo, Ma, for real—"

"Yo, Ma?" She said, clearly disgusted. "What's with all of this slang? You attend the prestigious and very expensive Maris Academy and this is how you're speaking? Please don't tell me my thousands of dollars a month in tuition are going down the drain."

OMG, has anybody else had enough of Diva Esquire? I turned to my father and pushed my Chanel-covered lips into a pout. "Daddy."

"Dee." He patted me on the head. "Cut Chance some slack."

"It's Dee*dra* and I really don't like her down there."

"Why don't you just say what you really mean!" Daddy snapped. "Just say you don't like her with my family! They don't live on the right side of town for you, Deedra?!"

"Did you just receive that memo, Mr. Kennedy?" She turned on her court room voice. "I told you *that* when you paraded her down there last year. And it's not that they don't live on the right side of town for me, they don't live on the right side of town for my child! I deal with Atlanta's thugs every day!"

As soon as she said that I knew it was on—which was cool for me, because their focus had shifted from me to one another.

But whatever, I didn't have time to stand around. I had a big night to prepare for and twenty minutes away from here was a whole other world, that, come hell or high water, I had to get to.

2

You wassup, girl . . .

—FABOLOUS, "YOU BE KILLIN' 'EM"

I drove into Bankhead in my bangin' ride with my Bose system pumpin' and a look so fly it was a struggle to describe—but I'll try.

My hair was flat-ironed straight and pulled back into a sleek ponytail that swung at least four inches past my shoulders. My ears were adorned in a platinum pair of large hoops that most probably thought were sterling silver, and my right arm was dressed with three chunky and different shades of pink sapphire bangles. Painted on my tight thighs and glued to my perfectly round bottom were black Roberto Cavalli skinny jeans. My full breasts sat up just right in a hot-pink halter—the same exact color of my car. And yes, oh yes, my four-inch, Christian Louboutin pink and patent-leather heels were serious. Make no mistake and never underestimate, my shoe game was tight.

I laid on the horn as I pulled up in front of Nana's house, where my crew, better known as the Thick-n-Juicy clique—named after our description of ripe Georgia peaches—waited for me.

Nana's house was where we always met up. It was the only place we could go and not be stressed. Mainly because Nana did her own thing and she encouraged us to do ours. There were only two things she didn't tolerate: disrespect and a nasty house. Outside of that we had free rein, which was the exact opposite of my house.

There was no way we could hang in Alpharetta. My mother wouldn't dare open her eight-thousand-square-foot, six-bedroom, and seven-bathroom mansion to the likes of Bankhead residents. And the only reason Keeya ever came over—and her visits were few and far between—was because she was family. Otherwise, she would've been on the outside of the electronic gate looking in. So, there wasn't a doubt in my mind that Riunite and Martini—named after their mother's favorite drinks—could never look her way.

There was also no way we'd make the mistake of hanging out at Ree-Ree and Martini's spot ever-ever-ever-again! Ever since their mother married a pastor, they have Saturday-night prayer service at their house. The last time we were there, their parents turned the living room into a church and made us testify and praise dance. All of which made Nana's house a unanimous decision.

I laid on the horn again and finally the screen door flew open.

"Daaaaang!" Martini spat in her extremely thick and heavy Georgian accent. "You took hella long! We been walkin' round on ten for two hours ready to get it crunked, and here you just showin' up! You better be lucky we're girls and this is your grandmama's house. Otherwise, it'd be a problem." She batted her extended lashes and placed her hands on her voluptuous hips. Her leopard mini dress crept up her thighs as she struggled to walk in her clear plastic stilettos. All I could do was roll my eyes to the sky, especially since Martini was the only one in our Thick-n-Juicy clique who insisted on wearing her clothes too small.

And she knew our constitution clearly stated: "There's a difference between bringing sexy back and needing to take yo behind back to the store for a bigger size." She also knew that since we were privileged to be big girls we had to be cute at all times. So why—oh why—she stuffed her size-fourteen body into a cheap, size-ten animal print getup was beyond me.

But you know what? It's my birthday and tonight it's about me and my ride so I'ma overlook her gear and let her live.

"Oh my!" Keeya screeched as she stepped onto the porch. She stamped her feet and her three-inch stilettos clapped against the wood planks like wind chimes. Keeya had flawless apple-butter skin and was a perfect size sixteen. We were pretty much shaped the same way: pear shaped with a flat middle. She wore a cute pair of jeggings, a sleeveless and white ruffle shirt, with a thick red leather belt wrapped around her waist. Her hair was cut into a layered one-sided bob and behind her right ear were cascading stars that ran down the side of her neck. She may have only been a year older than me, but I truly admired my aunty.

"Am I seeing right?" Keeya gushed. "Or am I seeing thangs?" She placed her hand over her eyes like a sun visor. "Is that my girl?" She pulled her round-eyed shades down the bridge of her nose.

"Yes, it is." Ree-Ree stepped from behind her and nudged Martini on the shoulder. Martini tried to hold out and not smile, but when I dropped the top and cranked up the hydraulics her face lit up and she screamed, "That ish is fiyah!"

"Make it hot!" Ree-Ree said as I turned the music up and hopped out the car. The rap group, Cali Swag District's "Teach Me How to Dougie" filled the air and as if on cue, we all chanted along with the song and started dancing. "You ain't messin' wit' my dougie!"

"Get it now!" Nana stepped onto the porch and smiled. Her green sponge rollers shook as she nodded her head to the beat. "Teach me how to Dougie!" she said with her arms opened wide. "Happy birthday, Nana's baby!"

My heels clicked up the stairs as I ran over to

Nana and hugged her tightly. She always had a way of making me feel five again, safe and secure like nothing else mattered but me. "You know Nana loves you!" She kissed me on my forehead. "And when you come back I have a gift for you."

"Awwl, thank you, Nana. You wanna hang with us?" I chuckled.

"Don't start nothin' now." She laughed. " 'Cause if I get out there with y'all and take all of this to the yard"—she ran her hands along the sides of her voluptuous body—"I'ma take all ya lil boyfriends, so you're better off leaving Nana home."

All I could do was fall into a deep and hearty laugh, mostly because I knew—with my grandmother's arms wrapped around me and my friends cranking up my birthday celebration by dancing the Dougie in the street—that it didn't get any better than this. This right here . . . and right now . . . was priceless.

We rode in on cloud nine and I felt like red carpet cushioned the tires as we made a right turn into McDaniel's parking lot, where instead of feeling like we'd just arrived at the neighborhood bowling alley, we felt like we'd arrived at the BET awards. And we were the stars. All eyes were most def on us as we parted the multicolored sea of vehicles, chicks, and lil daddies from all over the A. So, of course, we found a parking space in the center of everything.

"Big up to all my haters!" blasted from the four speakers, one on each corner of the bowling alley's roof. The DJ, who was inside of the building, but played music that also catered to the party in the parking lot, pumped Shawty Lo's "Dey Know" remix into the Sunday-night crowd.

The parking lot was pretty much an outdoor club. There was a spot to buy drinks, a soul-food stand, a spot where people congregated to dance, and in the center of everything was a congregation of fly rides.

McDaniel's was the truth, and judging by the way folks peeped out my Impala, I knew that they knew the custom-colored and kitted-up Messiah had finally arrived. Amen.

"Chance," Martini said, excited, "we have something for you." I glanced at her in my rearview mirror and she grinned from ear to ear. With the exception of her too-small clothes, Martini was a dead ringer for Raven-Symoné. Her skin was the color of honey and her hair hung to her shoulders in a fly and bouncy doobie.

"Really?" I said playfully. "Would it be in that box you tried to sneak out the house?"

"You are so nosey." Ree-Ree, who was the color of a crisp brown paper bag and rocked micro braids that framed her round face and hazel eyes perfectly, playfully smacked her lips and we all laughed.

I turned around to face the backseat, where

Martini and Ree-Ree were. "Divas, you didn't have to get me anything."

"You know how we do it," Keeya said. "Now open it!"

Martini handed me a gift-wrapped box with a white bow on top. She popped her lips and said, "Gurrrrrrrl, you gon' love it!" She exaggerated her words the way she always did when she was either mad or excited.

"I know I will," I said as I untied the white bow from around the wrapped box.

"I picked it out," Martini carried on.

"We all picked it out," Keeya said.

"Well, I saw it first," Ree-Ree insisted.

"But I took it to the register to pay for it." Martini snapped her fingers. "Now shut it down and let her open the thang."

I ripped the wrapping paper off and Martini said, "You want me to tell you what's in there?" Before I could say no, she popped her lips and continued, "Hon'ney, it's this fly white V-neck tee, that hangs off one shoulder with gold letters that read, 'Thick-n-Juicy!' "

"Could you let her open the box! Dang," Keeya snapped as I revealed the shirt. "You talk too much, Martini."

"Whatever." Martini dismissed her and carried on. "Chance, gurl, it's fly, right?"

"I love it!" I screamed.

"Bam!" Ree-Ree said. "You know we had to hook up our girl." She grinned.

"Now get to the rest," Martini rushed me. "Take the leggings out!"

Keeya and Ree-Ree shot Martini the evil eye, and she said, "I'm sorry. I'm just excited."

"It's cool," I said as I sorted through the tissue paper and pulled out a pair of glittering gold and psychedelic white zebra-print leggings. *What kinda . . . ?*

"What kind of nasty—" Keeya frowned. "Where did those come from?"

"Martini," Ree-Ree said, "that's not what we picked out! The ones we picked out were solid white!"

"And a size fourteen, I hope." I blinked in disbelief at the size six on the tag. "I haven't worn a size six since the third grade."

"A size six?" Keeya spat. "Martini, are you getting high? Do we need to get you some help?"

"Crack is whack." Martini rolled her eyes. "And anyway, I liked the zebra print, and the white and gold is what makes the pants sizzle."

"A sizzling mess," Keeya interjected. "No wonder you volunteered to stand in that long line while we went to get the shirt, 'cause you switched the pants."

"Well, Chance likes 'em," Martini said. "Tell her, Chance."

"Umm . . . well . . ." I stuttered. "Umm . . . well, they're too little."

"They are not too little, I buy a size six all the time," Martini said.

"And that's a problem!" Keeya rambled through her purse, and pulled out our constitution—and yes, we had a constitution. Don't get it twisted; Thick-n-Juicy was official. "Our constitution clearly states," Keeya continued, "to wear your damn size."

"Didn't I tell you that before we left home?" Ree-Ree spat.

"Looka here," Martini said defensively, "I'm reppin' sexy!"

"You reppin' crazy. You know you don't . . . need . . ." Ree-Ree said and her voice started to drift. "Wait a minute." She pointed. "Is that Hakeem, your boyfriend, Martini?" She blinked repeatedly.

Keeya and I turned around quickly and gawked out the windshield, and sure enough that was Martini's boyfriend.

"Oh, I'm 'bout to split that wig right down to the white meat!" Martini spat.

"Who are those two chicks he's with?" I asked and before anyone could respond, Derrell appeared seemingly out of nowhere and strolled over to Hakeem. Derrell gave Hakeem a fist bump, and then he took one of the chicks who stood next to Hakeem by the hand.

Let me say this slowly: My . . . mouth . . . dropped . . . wide . . . open. Especially since this hood bugger was the skinniest chick I'd ever seen and don't you know that this clown—Derrell—my man—peppered her lips with soft kisses and wrapped his arms around her waist.

"Oh . . . my . . . God . . ." we all said in unison.

"Three violations in one night!" Keeya spat, "Hakeem hugged up with some random chick and Derrell over there cupcakin', and on top of that, cupcakin' with some po' bone. One, two, three violations!" She turned to me. "Didn't you tell him"—she rattled the paper in her hand—"that our constitution clearly states that 'Skinny chicks are evil!' "

"Halle'looter!" Ree-Ree said. "Tell 'em!"

"That's why you don't see my boyfriend, Elijah, over there," Keeya said proudly. " 'Cause I would go straight karate kid all over him! Okay? Don't play with me. And Chance, it's your birthday and Derrell's over there in that pigeon's face?"

Ree-Ree put her two cents in—"Chance, you gon' let a scrub"—then she turned to Martini. "And Martini, you gon' let a hood rat play you?"

"You two"—Keeya wagged her index finger—"better go handle your scandals. And don't worry; we got your backs."

I couldn't believe my eyes. And here I thought Derrell was too busy stalking me to ever cheat. I mean, not that I was really into him, and yeah, he was a trial run but he didn't know that . . . and this is what he's been doing to me?

"Why you moving so slow?" Keeya spat. "We have a don't-tolerate-no-nonsense rep to protect."

I ignored Keeya and turned toward a glassy-eyed Martini. "Are you crying?"

"No," she sniffed. "I'm good."

"You better be good," I snapped. " 'Cause yeah, they playing us right now, and yeah, they lied to us, but no matter what, we don't drop no tears. 'Cause we are what?"

"Divas!" everyone said in unison.

I continued, "And when Thick-n-Juicy dismisses one hot boy—"

"We don't sweat it," we all said. "We move on to the next." We placed our left hands over our hearts and said, "We pledge allegiance to the Thick-n-Juicy flag that we will never be had." We snapped our fingers in a Z motion and made our catcall, "Thick-n-Juiceee!"

"Now." I popped my lips. "This is what we're going to do. We're going over there to tap them on the shoulders and let them know they've been busted. But we're not going to spaz or lose control. We're going to lay them out like the divas we are and keep it movin'. Agreed?"

"Agreed." Martini dabbed the corners of her eyes.

"Cool," I said as we eased out of the car and quietly closed our respective doors. We each glanced back at our reflection in the windows and once we silently confirmed that we were fly, we sauntered toward the pimp-playin' culprits. And no sooner than we made two clicks toward them, Martini screamed, "Haaaaaaakeeeeeeem! Yo azz is mine!"

Pause! OMG. No she didn't. I could've slapped her. Now we had no choice but to bring it, especially since one of our bylaws is "When one goes off, we all get amped!"

The closer we got to them, the wider Hakeem and Derrell's eyes grew. It was obvious they couldn't think of a lie quick enough, so their mouths simply dropped open while Martini continued her rant, "Ain't no need to run! And ain't no need to hide!"

"Tini, I can explain." Hakeem pushed the chick he had his arm wrapped around to the side of him. "See, what had happened was ummm . . . ummm . . . ummm—"

His ummm turned into a hum, because by the time I ripped into Derrell he was still on the same note. "So this is how we droppin' it?" I spat at Derrell. "This is what you been doing, carrying bones around?"

"Who you calling a bone?" the skinny chick snapped.

"You, Bone-queesha." Keeya looked her over. "She was most def talking to you. And what you gon' do?"

"That's not my name." The girl rolled her eyes.

"Then what is it?" I popped my neck from side to side. "Ho? Nasty? Freak? Home wrecker? Skeezer? 'Bout to get beat? Choose one."

"Derrell," the girl carried on, "you better tell her who I am! I'm Derrell's girl!"

"His girl?!" I screamed.

"Chance, listen," Derrell said, and I could've sworn he stuck his chest out. "Don't come over here with a buncha ra-ra, a'ight! You know the deal, so step off. Matter a fact, step away!"

Screech! Hold up . . . wait a minute. Did he *just . . . no, he didn't just say . . . oh yes, he did!* I blinked my eyes in complete disbelief, because apparently this fool had lost his mind beating his chest at me. For a moment, I thought about gut punching him, but then I thought about how I really didn't want to be out here scrapping and risk messing up my cuteness. So I settled on slapping him with my mouth. "I know you not over here trying to get beefy with me when you're the oldest kid in the eleventh grade. Did you tell this chicken how you're facing charges for selling bootleg DVDs?!"

"Bootleg DVDS?" the girl said in complete shock.

"Bootleg," my crew said in unison, "DVDs."

"And there we have it." I rolled my neck for emphasis. "But, Derrell, you up here trying to serve me? What you need to be is the lil girl you act like. 'Cause for-real for-real, I was doing the church of whackness a favor when I hooked up with you. But since you have found the first lady of hood-hos, maybe she can make a man out of you, 'cause we're through!" I flicked my hand like I'd just performed a magic trick.

Martini and Hakeem were still going at it, and Hakeem's sideline ho had stormed away, especially since he'd changed his whole lie and said he didn't know who the chick was or why she was standing next to him. Martini told Hakeem to get out of her face.

"I didn't think you wanted none." Keeya eyed Derrell's skank, and then we all, including Martini, made a motion as if we had dusted our shoulders off, put our oceans in motion, and sauntered away.

I couldn't believe what had just gone down. Once my clique and I reached my car, we sat on the hood and clicked our heels on the chrome grill. As we went to recap the drama we'd just handled, a loud blast of *Pop-pop-pop-Radda-tat-tat!* filled the air.

We looked at each other, and before any of us could completely process a thought, the gripping sound ripped through the air again.

Pop-pop-pop-Radda-tat-tat! Pop-pop-pop-Radda-tat-tat! Pop-pop-pop-Radda-tat-tat!

Instantly, I froze.

Pop-pop-pop-Radda-tat-tat!

I knew my clique had all hit the ground, but I couldn't move. This was crazy. I'd never been frozen like this. I was scared. I had to be. And no matter how many times my mother told me that Bankhead was not the place to be, I still never believed that I would be in the middle of bullets soaring like birds.

Pop-pop-pop-Radda-tat-tat!

Before my mind could let go of the shock I felt my body hit the ground and a loud thud rang in my ears. Suddenly my chest felt heavy and there was no doubt in my mind that I'd been shot.

"You all right, ma?"

Where did that come from?

I blinked and that's when I realized that pressed on top of me was a chocolate knight, with a face so fine that for a moment I thought maybe I'd died and had gone to heaven.

Pop-pop-pop-Radda-tat-tat!

"I'm . . . I'm . . ." I stuttered. "I'm . . . ummm . . . okay."

He didn't respond. And within a matter of seconds the bullets stopped singing, the air became silent and instantly the crowd erupted, car tires screeched, and the smell of burning rubber filled the air.

"Ahmad," someone shouted, "come on!" and just like that my knight was gone. No good-bye, nothing. Just like that he disappeared.

"You okay, Chance?" A tearful Keeya asked. "I thought you were on the ground with us and when I didn't see you—" She broke out into tears.

"I'm okay, Keeya," I said, stunned. My eyes roamed from one side of the parking lot to the other trying to see if I saw this guy anywhere. "Did you see that guy?"

"What guy?" Keeya dried her eyes.

"Listen," Ree-Ree said, "we don't have time to talk about a guy. We have to get out of here."

"You're right, let's go!" I said and as I hopped

off the ground I spotted a white gold chain with a basketball charm hanging on it. My eyes scanned the parking lot again and Ree-Ree yelled, "I'll drive! You're still in shock." She snatched the keys from my hand and we all hurriedly piled in the car and took off.

3

I hope she cheats on you with a basketball player . . .

—MARSHA, "I HOPE SHE CHEATS ON YOU"

I'ma keep it one hundred. The random shoot-out at McDaniel's had me shook, but nothing was worse than Derrell popping his collar and trying to play me. I promise you, I hadn't been played like that since the ninth grade when my cell phone bill was a thousand dollars; my mother revoked my texting privileges and restricted my outgoing calls to her phone and 911. Now, that was some ish, but I do believe Derrell getting caught with Frail-derella and then talking greasy out the side of his neck had my mother's punishment beat hands down.

So, why he stood at Nana's screen door begging to come inside was beyond me, 'cause there was no way he was getting up in here. Zero. Zilch. Nada. And that decision had nothing to do with my feelings being hurt; it was solely based on pride.

"Read my lips." I cracked the screen door open wide enough so that he could see my mouth move without the mesh obscuring his view. "You better get on!" Then I let the screen door's wooden frame slam in his face. "Now pick ya lip up and walk away."

"Chance, listen to me—"

"Listen to you?" I blinked in disbelief. "I heard you last night when you told me to step off and then you went in for the kill and said, 'Matter fact, step away.' So yeah, umm-hmm, I've already listened to you. I heard you loud and clear. *And* you get caught cheating on my birthday? Who does that?"

"Look, I know I hurt you—"

"You didn't hurt me. You pissed me off, is what you did. Seriously, don't you know I've been trying to kick you to the left for a minute now?"

"I'm not going anywhere. And I know you don't mean anything you're saying. I can see the tears in your eyes, so you may as well forgive me and get to loving me again."

Oh . . . heck . . . no! Had he lost his mind? There were no tears in my eyes. And did he really think I wanted to be booed up with him again? Was he sick? Yeah, maybe this required me to step from behind the door, onto the porch, and stand directly in his face.

I pushed the screen door open, placed my hands on my hourglass hips, cocked my neck to the side, and at the very moment my mouth twisted and I was about to rip him, I noticed a familiar cutie across the street shooting hoops. By the time the cutie made a three-point play, I realized who he was: my chocolate knight.

OMG.

Suddenly, I was speechless. The vision before my eyes had to be the king of cuties or maybe he was even higher than that; maybe he was their god. He easily stood six-foot-three, was double-dipped in the world's most exclusive dark chocolate, and was equipped with a body that every cutie ought to have. He wore an Atlanta University sleeveless basketball jersey, a matching pair of basketball shorts, and a pair of crisp white Nikes.

I thought quickly of how I needed to be on the basketball court cheerleading, but then "Chance, you know I love you and I know you love me" brought me back to reality. I shook my head and stole another glance before I looked back into Derrell's face. The American dream was still across the street and the sound of his dribbling ball made love to my ears.

"Chance, forgive me." Derrell moved in for a kiss and I took two steps back. Apparently his small mind had him trippin' . . . again.

I took a deep breath. "Fa-real, fa-real, Derrell, you're tired. You were supposed to be a trial run, but you've exceeded your expiration date. Now step off." I flicked my hand. "No, excuse me, step away."

"Chance, I know you don't mean that."

"Boy, please lose yourself!"

"Look, I need to—"

"Kick rocks. Yeah, that's it, you need to take yo broke-down and busted behind over to where your lil Walmart freak lives and flap your gums at her doorstep. Now hurry, run along!"

Derrell blinked. "Who are you talking to, Chance?" He moved up close to me and the veins in his neck stuck out like lightning.

"You tryna get jumped up in this mother? You better fall back."

"All the way back," Keeya snapped from the living room window.

"Plus," I said, "I'm sure Tricka-rella doesn't want you sweatin' me."

"She was only a friend—"

"Puhlease." I yawned. "I did tell you you were tired, right?"

"So you don't want to be with me anymore. Is that what you're saying?"

"Did you just receive that memo, Mr. Johnson?" *Oh no, why did my mother's voice just scream in my head? Now I knew for sure this bearrilla had to leave.* So when he didn't move, I said, "You need me to translate 'get-ta-steppin'' into another language besides English?"

"You'll never find anybody as good as me!"

"Great, I have something to look forward to, because I don't want anybody as good as you. I need a step above whack."

"You know what," Derrell spat, "I'm done wit' you!"

I wiped invisible sweat from my brow. "Whew, finally, he gets it."

Derrell stood there for a moment and I could tell he struggled to leave, so I spat this out in hopes of helping him. "Deuces."

He didn't say anything; he simply stormed off the porch, got in his car, and took off.

I looked back across the street and the cutie was still there. After standing there for a few minutes to make sure Derrell wasn't doubling back, I knew now was the time to make my move. "Nana and Keeya, I'll be back!" I ran down the stairs and across the street.

Once I stood a few feet away from my mission, I stopped running. I didn't want to be breathing heavy with sweat drizzling like Crisco over my face. I had to keep my flyness intact, and especially in front of chocolate charming.

My stomach flipped into a series of knots as my mind rehearsed just what I would say.

I did my best to relax my shoulders as I walked onto the court and stood cattycorner of the towering black iron basketball hoop. Once I got his attention, I opened my arms wide as a signal for him to toss me the ball.

He stopped his dribbling midway, tucked the

ball under his arm, stood up straight, and looked at me. He was definitely six-foot-three.

His eyes roamed all over me . . . twice . . . from the half smile, half blush on my face, to my white V-neck and fitted tee, to my dark denim booty shorts with the fringe hem, to the designer kicks on my feet. I knew I'd caught him completely off guard so to break the ice, I said, "What? You don't play with girls?"

His luscious lips slanted to a one-sided grin and he said, "Nice to see that you're still alive." He tossed me the ball. "You came to say thank you?"

"Thank you?" I said in disbelief as I caught the ball and started to dribble. "If anything, I was thinking you owed me an apology."

"Apology?" He reached for the ball, but I hit him with a spin and took a quick shot. "Apology for what?" he asked.

The ball swooshed through the hoop and he grabbed it before I could. He stretched his long and muscular arm out before me and I noticed his tattoo of a green-eyed panther on his left bicep. We continued our dance and I said, "You should say sorry for knocking me down. You didn't have to fall on me that hard."

He chuckled. "A bullet hits a lot harder."

"True," I said, trying to snatch the ball. "So, I guess I should say thank you."

"Yeah, you should." He held the ball in the air. "Stop reaching." He took a scoring shot and dribbled the ball again.

"Reaching? What are you talking about?" I said, doing my best to distract him as I ducked beneath his arm, stole the ball, and made a shot. When the ball fell from the netted basket and into the palms of my cupped hands, I said, "You left without saying good-bye."

He stood completely still and silent for a moment; then he broke out into laughter. "Are you serious? Look, lil Miss Suburbia, keep this in mind the next time you hear bullets—hit the ground. 'Cause you only get one time for me to save you."

Dead. I didn't know what offended me more, his laughter or him calling me lil Miss Suburbia. I was far from lil Miss Suburbia. "Oh, wow, maybe you didn't know, but there's only one Chris Rock and Eddie Murphy's old . . . so . . . you may want to reconsider being a comedian." I parked my neck to one side and twisted my lips the opposite way, but underneath it all I was embarrassed and needed to break out of there.

"Slick between the lips, huh?" He smiled. "Pretty and deliciously thick, but slick between the lips. And ungrateful, too."

"Look, I just came to return your necklace." I removed it from my back pocket. "Not to be insulted. Now, if you think I'ma stand here for another round of your corny stand-up, you're wrong."

He snickered a little and then gave me a smile that could easily melt a million hearts. "Look, lil ma, I didn't mean any harm."

"Lil ma?" I frowned. "Look, lil whoadie, my name is Chance—" I paused. This whole deal had gone south with the quickness, and the sarcasm between my lips flowed easy and free like a cold breeze.

He said, "My fault. Chance, I'm Ahmad." And a few seconds later he fell out laughing again.

I promise you I wanted to gut him like a fish. "What's so funny?"

"You." His eyes scanned me. "You're too cute to be frowning and we don't know each other well enough for you to be mad at me."

"Whatever." I fought with all I could not to blush. "Nobody told you to run around here try-ing to be Superman. I didn't ask you to save me, and judging by the bruise on my back from you jumping on top of me, you weren't even that good at it."

I could tell by the look on his face that I'd ticked him off. "Well, how about this," he said. "I'll stop being Superman and the next time your par-ents let you out to rep the hood, don't play on the devil's playground."

Rep the hood? Play? Oh . . . hell . . . to the no . . . ! No he didn't. Did he just diss me? I walked up close to him, and the only thing between us was air and my opportunity to check him. "First of all, I don't do crazy. Trust me, I cut first and check for a heartbeat later. Second of all, I'm grown and my parents haven't *let me* play anywhere in a long time. And the next time you come out your mouth lopsided, I'ma take it to your throat, college boy." I dropped the ball from my grip and it rolled to the other side of the court. I turned on my heels and walked quickly toward Nana's house. My heart pounded a thousand miles a minute when I realized that I still had his necklace in my hand. I started to toss it across the street, but quickly changed my mind, especially since I was even more turned on by him now than I was before I walked over there.

Ugg!

4

This feeling inside . . .
I'm off the meter . . .

—CIARA, "C.R.U.S.H."

It had been five days, three hours, and forty-five minutes since I'd been a damsel in distress, which was code for hot mess. There was an anxious storm in my stomach for an arrogant hottie who for all intents and purposes I shouldn't have been able to stand . . . but my thoughts couldn't get enough of him.

It wasn't as if I didn't have other things in my life that should've taken up space in my thoughts, like how I hadn't seen my daddy since my birthday and had only seen my mother in passing—but *nooo*, I didn't trip off of always being left alone at home, I was too busy being captivated by a stupid bunch of "what if I see him again."

Ugg!

Besides, this cat could have a girl. And how about . . . I don't even really know this dude!

Hmph, I'm not the ebony version of Snow White and he is certainly no Prince Charming. I mean, he's cute, and tall, and dark, and brave, with the smoothest skin . . . tightest muscles . . . and a smile that could melt sun, but still, he ain't all that.

I held his necklace in the palm of my hand, placed it on my chest, and fell straight back on the bed. This was some bull!

A few minutes into my thoughts my iPhone rang. It was Martini. "Thick-n—" I answered.

"Juiceeeeee!" she completed our greeting. "Wassup, gurl? What it do? What it look like?"

"Okay," I said, amused, "you can calm down."

"Deeeeeeva, I got something to tell you!"

"What? And don't tell me you're back with Ha-keem!"

"Screeeeeech, the madness has been recalled. I don't do dogged. Hakeem is so yesterday I don't even know what year I left him in. Now, listen, I met this new lil daddy. And he was so cute and so sweet that standing next to him felt like I'd drowned in sugar."

"Where'd you meet him? Ree-Ree hooked you up?"

"Excuse you," she said, sounding offended. "Martini can find her own man, why do I need a hook-up? 'Cause I'm the chubby one? Huh?"

"What?"

"Big girls don't need a sympathy hook-up. Trust me, I can get my own hot tamale, Grandma!"

"Grandma? Martini!" I yelled into the phone. "Martini!"

"What?" I could clearly envision her eyes blinking like crazy.

"Bring it back, girl, bring it back."

"I'm back, diva, I'm back."

"You okay?"

"I'm good, girl. My fault for flipping. But something you said just reminded me of my grandmother. You know she tries to step to me when she comes here from Tennessee. I can't stand that old bitty and her Polident tricks."

"Oh . . . kay. But you just scared me."

"I'm straight, girl. I just had to get that off my chest. Anywho, back to my new boo. He is not a Ree-Ree hook-up. Ree-Ree's taste is hella nasty. Did you see that dude she dated last week? A Depend fell out of his backpack, diva. Messed . . . me . . . up!"

"What?! A Depend?"

"Can you imagine what those diapers smell like? A wreck. So no, Ree-Ree can't ever hook me up. I found my own Tootsie Roll. I met him yesterday on the basketball court."

I hesitated. "On the basketball court?"

"Yes, and I swear he was so fine, he had Gucci Mane beat."

"Gucci Mane?" I curled my lips. "Who told you he was fine?"

"Stop playing with me, you know Gucci is

'bout it. And so is my future boo. This cat is super-
natural fine. I just might work some roots on him
so I can be sure to keep him the rest of my life."

I cracked up laughing.

"Diva," she continued, "he's so fine I just might
wear my size. Psych, he wasn't that fine. But you
get the picture."

I was hesitant, but I had to ask this question.
"What was his name?"

"Farad."

I paused, completely stopped in my tracks.
"Did you say, Ahmad?"

"No, Farad."

*Close enough. I wonder if Ahmad is over there
macking on the court and tossing out random
names to whatever girl comes his way.* "What
does he look like, Martini?"

"Tall, light skin with a sexy bald head, girl."

"A bald head, not a crew cut?"

"Nope."

"And he's light skinned like Chris Brown and
not chocolate like Shawty Lo."

"Chris Breezy all the way."

Okay, now I could get amped. "Hey'yay, cutie
in the house. So when are you going out with
him?"

"Saturday. We're going to meet at Club Abyss."

"What?" I said in disbelief. "You have to be
twenty-one and over to get up in there."

"And?"

"And? How are we going to get up in there? We're only sixteen and I just turned sixteen."

"Girl, we're from Bankhead. We got this."

"I hope so."

"Trust me. Thick-n-Juicy will be in the building!"

"All right." I paused. "OMG, what the heck am I going to wear?!" I said, excited. I hopped off my bed and walked into my closet. I pulled out a few outfits and tossed them across my chaise. "What you gon' wear, Martini?"

"I don't know. I got this tiger-print dress I bought the other day."

"Another animal print?" I curled my lips in disgust.

"And you know it." Martini carried on, "It's sexy, and I have these yellow plastic heels—"

"Plastic?"

"Where are you going?" My mother peeked into my room and interrupted my conversation.

"I'm on the phone," I snapped.

"You talking to me?" Martini asked.

"No," I said, "I'm talking to my mom."

"Dang, you can say that to your mother? And say it like that? The only thing missing was you kicking up dust and saying, 'Now get on!'"

"Chance," my mother snapped, "I think you better watch your tone!" and she stormed away from my door.

Whatever.

"And that's all your mother's going to say?" Martini said, impressed.

"Please." I twisted my mouth. "I'm grown. I don't play that."

"Hmph," Martini said. "Well, I got you beat by six months, so that means I'm grown too." She paused. "Yeah, I'm grown too," she confirmed. "And Barbara bet not bring her butt up in here talking to me crazy while I'm on the phone or it will be a problem."

"Martini, I don't think you need to be—"

"Wait a minute, Chance," she said, "here she comes right now and I know she's going to have something to say."

"Martini Alizé!" Martini's mother, Ms. Barbara, shouted. "Don't you have some chores to do? How long you gon' be on that phone?"

"Until I get off!"

Silence. Complete silence. I couldn't believe it. Ms. Barbara didn't say anything. Not a word. And here I thought she wasn't the type to play. I knew my mother tolerated my mouth because I'd pretty much raised myself and she felt hella guilty about that, but Ms. Barbara?

"Yeah," Martini said into the phone, "I'ma stop her from interrupting my conversations. She's too much in my Kool-Aid—"

"Martini," I said, still shook, "I think you better be quiet."

"Diva, please, I'm grown. I washed the dishes, I

cleaned up my room, what more she want? Hmph, she takes things around here to new heights and—"

Ahhhh . . . !!!! Bop, bop, bop, ahhhh . . . !!!! 45
Rumble, rumble, rumble . . . ahhhh . . . !!!! Ding!

What the heck was that? "Martini . . . Martini . . . Mar-teeeeeneeeee! Hello . . . hellooo . . ." I sang into the phone, and when no one answered, I tapped on the phone and screamed, "Martini!"

"Chance, this is Ree-Ree."

"What happened to Martini?"

"She needs to call you back; she's not breathing right now. I think my mother killed her." *Click.*

Dang. I looked at the clothes sprawled across my chaise and instead of wondering what I was going to wear to a party, I wondered what I would wear to Martini's funeral.

5

Baby, you got what I want . . .

—MISSY ELLIOTT, "HOT BOYZ"

"Chance." Keeya popped her gums as we huddled in her bedroom mirror and glamorized our faces to china-doll perfection. "You need to hurry and get dressed. In a minute, we're going to miss our opportunity to make a grand entrance. We'll just be considered late as hell."

"And we can not sacrifice a grand entrance," Ree-Ree insisted.

"I sure wish I could go," Martini said, somberly. "But I've been placed on lockdown for a year." Tears filled her eyes. "And I was gonna wear this half-tiger, half-leopard-print mini dress to the fullest! Chance," she sniffed, "you wanna rock this for me?" She pulled the dress from her purse.

I was totally disgusted. "Heck no!" I looked at her in disbelief. "I don't wear a size six—and neither do you. So give it up. And furthermore, if your mother let you come out the house to hang with us at Nana's, how would she know if you went to a party?"

"Seriously," Keeya said. "I was thinking the same thing."

"You don't even have to stay that long," Ree-Ree encouraged.

Martini hesitated. "I don't know, y'all." She paused. "You really don't think she'll notice?"

"Nope." I grabbed my sleeveless black mini dress. "Not at all."

Martini sat on the edge of Keeya's bed for a few moments. Her face looked as if she was sorting through a zillion thoughts, and then she said, "Okay, as long as we stay about an hour, two at most. Long enough for me to kick it with my boo for a minute."

"All right." A smile lit up my face. "Get dressed. We have a grand entrance to make."

"And besides"—Martini popped her lips—"I have the IDs we need to get in there."

"Martini." I sucked my teeth as we parked in the club's parking lot. "What kinda fake IDs are these? Who is this girl?"

"That's Lucille from down the street." Martini smacked her lips together.

"Crackhead Lucille!" I couldn't believe this. "I don't look like a crackhead!"

"And you don't look twenty-one either. Now, I

need my ten dollars back for that ID. She charges a rental fee."

"A rental fee? You rented IDs? I don't believe this, and from Lucille of all people?"

"Well, at least Lucille is in her twenties," Ree-Ree said. "Hmph, my person is sixty years old!"

"That's Lucille's mama," Martini said. "All she wanted in exchange for her ID was some brown liquor—whatever that is—but she needs that ID back tomorrow. She has to go to the Social Security office."

"O . . . M . . . G . . ." Keeya said, shaking her head. "Why is there a man on my ID?"

"That's Lucille's brother. She told me he liked to wear dresses on the weekend, so I figured that was close enough. Your ID was only five dollars, Keeya."

"I'm not paying for this!"

"Look a-here," Martini snapped, "get it together, Thick-n-Juicy. I did my part. I rented the IDs and got us on our way to the flyest party on this side of the A, and all you three can do is complain? I'm the one on punishment! I'm risking my life, 'cause you know if Barbara catches me out here, she will beat the future outta me!"

"True," we all said in reluctant uniformity.

"So stop complaining and let's get this party started!"

My heart pounded like crazy as we swayed toward the velvet rope where the bouncers carded the partygoers. We flashed the ridiculous IDs we had, and a few seconds later the bouncers lifted the rope and let us into heaven. No questions asked, and the only thing they said was, "Enjoy your night, ladies."

I couldn't believe this. I'd snuck into a few places where you had to at least be eighteen . . . but a club for twenty-one and over was a whole other level.

Club Abyss was hot too: white leather seats, all-glass bar, and a dance floor with glowing indigo tiles.

We were certainly in the place to be. The crowd was right and the music was tight. It didn't take long for my girls and I to rear our shoulders back and get our grown and sexy on. "Martini!" The shout rose above the club's mixed chatter. We turned around and a tall, honey-colored and muscled-down hottie waved at Martini from across the room. "Right here."

"There's my boo," Martini squealed. We followed her as she walked swiftly toward him. And judging from the up down he gave her, they were diggin' each other equally.

"Farad, these are my girls." Martini smiled. She introduced us by name and said, "They're here by themselves and need some hook-ups. Now"—she popped her lips—"where your friends at? I don't want my girls out here all lonely and desperate."

Did she say lonely? And desperate?

"I got you, ma," he said, winking his eye at Martini. "Give me a minute." And he stepped away. As soon as he was out of earshot, we ripped into this chick.

"I have a boyfriend!" Keeya spat. "I didn't ask you to hook me up."

"Y'all been together for two years, Keeya," Martini said. "Er'body needs a change."

"And I'm not lonely," Ree-Ree said defensively. "Or desperate."

"You may not be lonely, but you're desperate." Martini nodded her head. " 'Cause when that Depend fell out of that dude's bag, I viewed you in a whole other light."

"You buggin'," I said. "Straight buggin'."

We all stood there with our arms folded across our breasts and serious attitudes reflected on our faces.

"Ladies," Farad walked back over to us and said, "these are my friends."

Suddenly all of our attitudes disappeared and we were all in. They were the epitome of Hot Boyz, just the way we liked 'em.

I can't recall the exact moment that my crew and I split up into couples. All I knew was that Keeya and her dude were slow dancing, Martini was boo-macking in the corner, and judging by the intense look on Ree-Ree's face, she was already confessing to her cutie the zillion ex-boyfriend tales about what she was and wasn't going to tolerate.

But the hottie standing next to me . . . was a

loser. Why did he ask me did I have tracks in my hair? And when I said no, he stuck his nasty hand—without asking me—through my ponytail. It took everything in me not to steal on him. Instead, I sat like a stupid bump on a barstool and tried to think of ways to shake him. "You drink?" he asked me, and I blinked twice, which I guess is why he asked me again. "You drink? Would you like a glass of wine?"

I didn't even know how to respond to that. So I didn't. I nodded my head to the music and moved my hips lightly on the stool.

This was about to be a problem.

He took a sip of his Heineken and said, "That's cool, you don't have to answer. That means I can spend more money on me."

Oh no, he didn't.

"You don't talk much, do you?" he asked. "What does a brother need to do to get you to open up?"

What you need to do is get out my face, especially since along with you being stooopid, your breath stinks. Got a Tic Tac? "I'm a little quiet. At least until I get to know you."

"I understand that." He sipped. "So, is there anything I can get you?"

"Know what? I think I just want a peppermint. Something tells me we need some mints around here."

"Word?" this creep said. "Oh a'ight. So you a cheap date, huh? You in a club and all you want are mints. I bet you if I took you out to eat, you'd probably order a number five or something." And then he laughed.

I blinked. Not once, but twice. Because I could've sworn that spit just flew from between this monster's lips. How do we spell disaster? I couldn't take it anymore. "Look, umm"—I snapped my fingers, realizing I didn't know his name—"umm . . . ummm . . ."

"It's Ahmad." A familiar voice traveled from behind me. "I told you that the other day."

"What?" A smile bloomed on my face and I couldn't stop grinning.

"'Scuse me, pot'nah," the cat who'd been ruining my life for the past ten minutes said to Ahmad. "Is this you?" He pointed to me.

"Umm-hmm," I volunteered. "That's what I was trying to tell you, Stanley," I said, taking a guess at what his name could be.

"It's Otis."

"Stanley, Otis, same thing. But anyway, this is my man."

Ahmad slid his arms around my waist and whispered in my ear, "You owe me." He looked at Otis and said, "Sorry, man. But seems all the good ones are taken."

"Whatever," Otis snapped. "She's a cheap date anyway." And he walked swiftly away from us. Ahmad smiled at me and not only did it light up the room, but it sent the butterflies in my stomach into overdrive. "Are you stalking me?" I asked him.

"That's a good question." His eyes roamed my body. "I was going to ask you the same thing."

"Whatever." I blushed like crazy. I knew I looked ridiculous.

"So, how should we do this?"

"Do what?" I said as I fought my blush from turning into a full smile.

"Do you wanna pick up the argument from when we last saw each other, or do you wanna start from this moment—where you're feeling me and I'm clearly feeling you." He softly stroked my cheek. "It's up to you."

I wasn't sure if I'd still be able to speak, being that I'd pretty much melted in my seat. "I think"— I swallowed—"I'd like to start from this moment."

6

Oh you fancy, huh?

—DRAKE, "FANCY"

I hated sushi. Hated it. And no, I'd never tried it. It was just one of those foods that always sounded nasty. Raw fish wrapped in seaweed and rice. Need I say more? But for a dream date with Ahmad, I would put my reservations to the side and try it, just once.

Butterflies fluttered wildly in my stomach as I stood in the middle of Keeya's bedroom floor and changed into five different outfits. It would've been six had Martini not said, "Daaaaang, you on it like that, diva?" That's when I realized I was a little too hyped for this date tonight. From the time I turned from fiery fifteen to sweet sixteen, I'd had my share of dates at movies, clubs, fish fries, and jumpin' parking lots. So, there was really no need for me to be this excited . . . or was it anxious? But whatever it was, I needed to shake it.

"No." I tossed a quick look over my shoulder toward Martini. "I am not on it at all. I mean, he's cute and everything, but ummm, I only attract cuties. So he's a free meal, nothing more, nothing less."

"A free meal?" Ree-Ree frowned. "You don't even like sushi." She parked her lips to the side.

"So what? I'm willing to try it, and we're going to listen to some jazz." I spun around and pointed my index finger at them. "See, y'all don't know nothin' about that."

"Oh, you fancy, huh?" Martini smacked her lips. "Girl, please, you know you're the queen of the Bankhead Bounce."

They fell out laughing and despite the fact that the look on my face clearly said that I didn't find them amusing, they carried on. "If ya thick," Martini sang, "turn around and shake ya wits!"

They each popped up and off the bed and as soon as their bare feet hit the floor, they put down the Bankhead Bounce like nobody's business. *Ugg!* I wanted to be pissed, but all I could do was laugh. "Y'all wrong for that," I said as I broke into the Bounce with them. Afterward, we fell across the bed and I let out a long and hard sigh. "What am I going to wear?"

"Look." Keeya sat up and pointed to the heap of clothes I'd created on the floor. "Put that passion-purple strapless dress on. It fits you like a glove and shows off your hourglass."

"You think?"

"Yeah," Ree-Ree said, "that one looked real cute on you."

"It was a'ight." Martini smacked her lips. "But me, personally, I would throw on a fake fur, a leopard bodysuit, some Cinderella platforms, and put 'em all to sleep! He would be like, 'Is that Martini Alizé Sherell?'"

We paused, and at the very moment when it seemed that at least one of us would address the madness that Martini just dropped in the air, we resumed talking about my date. "So what time are you supposed to meet him?" Keeya asked.

I glanced at the clock. "Oh my God, I was supposed to be there twenty minutes ago!"

"Dear God," I prayed as I sat in the parking lot at Arriang's Jazz and Sushi House. "Puhlease"—I shook my hands in a prayer position—"bless me not to act goofy, say something totally stupid, or eat too much. Especially since this dress can't hold another inch. Amen."

I sucked in my stomach and hoped it would tame the wild butterflies. Otherwise, I would feel too jumpy and would never be able to work my three-inch stilettos and rock my fitted dress correctly. I tucked my clutch beneath my arm, sucked in a deep gulp of air, and slowly released it out the center of my mouth.

My reflection sparkled in the all-glass entrance as I walked into the restaurant. This place was absolutely beautiful and reminded me of the spots my mother and father would take me to, on the rare moments they felt connected. Each table was a secluded booth that could easily have privacy by drawing the velvet curtains on the sides of the individual booths together.

The hostess greeted me. "Welcome."

"Thank you," I said as I tried to remember how my mother always said to ask for people you were waiting for at a restaurant. "My party should already be here. Mr. Ahmad King."

"Yes." She nodded. "Mr. King is expecting you."

The hostess led the way. We passed a live jazz band that played Boney James's "R.S.V.P." I nodded my head to the beat all the way to our table. I wasn't sure if Ahmad noticed me coming his way or not. Dressed in a pair of slightly baggy jeans, a navy-blue blazer with a Ralph Lauren crest on the breast's pocket, and a crisp white tee underneath, he was combing the menu. His swagger was Swizz Beatz and Jay-Z, serious. The only thing missing was his gold chain, which I had yet to return to him.

"Mr. King," the hostess called for his attention.

Ahmad looked up and my reflection filled his eyes.

"Your server will be over shortly," the hostess said and then she left.

"Chance." Ahmad stood up to greet me. "You look wonderful."

"Thank you." I smiled. "And so do you."

He sat back down. "I brought these for you." He handed me a bouquet of red roses.

I gasped and then I squealed, "They're beautiful." I knew I'd promised myself that I would keep my smiling to a minimum, but there was no way I could fight the sinking of my dimples. My heart jumped double Dutch in my chest as I pinched my thigh to make sure this wasn't a dream. Who would ever think that as much as Thick-n-Juicy kept it hood that I would end up on a date like this? This was something straight out of the movies. "Thank you so much!"

"You're so welcome."

"Wait, I have something for you too," I said, pulling a white jewelry box from my purse. "It's your necklace. I got it fixed for you, Superman."

Ahmad's eyes seemed to sparkle and I swear, I think he was the cutest guy on Earth. "Thank you," he said as I handed him the box and he slid the chain back around his neck.

A few minutes into us basking in the glee of the gifts we'd exchanged, the band changed their tune to a Chuck Loeb classic and before I realized it, I hummed along.

"Jazz fan?" Ahmad asked me.

I hated that I blushed, again. "Yes. I love jazz. My dad has an extensive collection. I grew up listening to it."

His smile lit up the place. "I'm a big fan myself; actually my father is a jazz musician. He owns a club in Harlem."

"In Harlem?" I said, impressed. "Really? A musician? Do you play?"

"I mess with the piano some, but my brother, now he kills it."

"Is your family in Atlanta or New York?"

"New York," he said as the server approached our table. "I'm the only one here in Atlanta."

The Japanese waitress bowed and said, "May we start you with a glass of wine this evening?"

"Oh no." I shook my head, and chuckled nervously. "No thank you. I'll just have a Sprite."

"Sounds good." Ahmad smiled. "Same for me. Chance, are you ready to order?"

I hesitated, especially since I didn't know what to order. Heck, I didn't eat sushi. "Ummm, you order for me."

"Okay," he said and then placed our order. After the server walked away he returned his attention to me and said, "Would you like to dance?" He pointed toward the small dance floor near the band. There were a few couples dancing and having a good time. Honestly, I was hesitant, but then I figured, *why not?* "Sure," I said, "I'd love to dance."

Ahmad took me by the hand and led me to the dance floor, where we grooved through three tunes. Thick-n-Juicy wouldn't believe their eyes if they saw me busting another move besides poppin' and droppin' it.

By the time we retook our seats, the server

brought us our food and laid it out on the table for us.

"Would you like me to draw the curtains too?" she asked.

"Sure." Ahmad smiled. "Thank you."

The server left and Ahmad said to me, "You're a great dancer."

"Thank you." I placed my napkin across my lap. "And you're not too bad yourself."

"Not too bad?" He chuckled a bit. "Oh word? That's it, I'm not too bad?"

I cracked up. "I knew it."

"Knew what?" He dipped his sushi in soy sauce.

"I knew you had some b-boy in you." I started to eat my salad.

"I'm from New York, baby. I can b-boy all day. But when I'm with a beautiful young lady such as yourself, I need her to know that she's on a date with a man, and not her homie."

Did I die and somebody forgot to tell me? Because surely I was in heaven.

"But maybe on another date," he continued, "we can represent."

"Bet." I nodded my head in agreement. "I'ma take you somewhere and show you how we handle things in Hotlanta."

He cracked up. "What you gon' be, my tour guide?"

"And you know this," I said, taking sneak peeks at the sushi not quite sure what to try.

"A'ight, straight."

"So," I asked him, still staring at the sushi, "which one should I try?" I pointed to the sushi platter.

"You never had sushi?" He arched his brow.

"Not exactly. Me and the whole raw-fish thing—"

"All of it's not raw." He pointed to a roll. "That's shrimp tempura. The shrimp is fried. Taste it." He took my chopsticks, picked up the roll, dipped it in soy sauce and fed it to me. "Hmmm." I chewed, slowly. "That was delicious." He fed me another and before long I'd tried all sorts of sushi rolls.

"How'd you end up in Atlanta if your family is from New York?" I asked, Ahmad, now controlling my own chopsticks.

"School," he said. "I wanted to attend the University of Atlanta. They had one of the best accounting programs in the country. And having a full academic scholarship also helped drive the point home of which school I needed to choose."

I chuckled. "I can understand that. What year are you in?"

"My senior year."

Don't ask me why, but I attempted to calculate his age. When I couldn't exactly figure out if he was twenty or twenty-one, I asked him, "How old are you?"

"Twenty-two."

What?! Damn!

"And you?" he asked.

Sixteen. "Umm, eighteen." I knew at the exact

moment the lie rolled off my tongue and parted my lips that I shouldn't have told it. Yet, I prayed like hell he didn't pick up my hesitation or better yet, doubt me.

"Eighteen?" he said, taken aback. "So you and your girls were in the club just kickin' it? It didn't even matter that it was for twenty-one and over. Let me find out you got game." He chuckled a bit and I did too, except mine was phony.

"Me being eighteen, is that a problem?" I asked.

"Nah, it's cool. Now, any younger than that, I would be like listen, I don't mac at the daycare."

Not knowing what else to say or follow up with, I said, "Sooo . . . you're really into accounting, huh?"

"Yeah. Actually, I have a double major, accounting and business management. I'm taking a few summer classes. How about you? Are you in school?"

"Of course," I said nervously, praying he didn't ask me where.

"Where do you go?"

I guess God missed that prayer. Think . . . think . . . think . . . "Umm, I attend Atlanta Community College."

"What year?"

"Freshman. Yeah, freshman."

"Are you taking any summer courses?"

"No." The first truthful thing, besides my name, I've said all night. "My classes resume in the fall."

"What classes will you be taking?"

"Ummm . . . gym—"

He gave me a slight grin and a small chuckle. "Gym? What?"

"I'm joking." I struggled to laugh.

"Ma, you're a trip. Gym." He shook his head. "You had me for a minute there."

Yeah, you ain't the only one feeling had.

"Now, seriously," he pressed. "What classes are you taking?"

"Sociology and, umm, psychology. A few here and there. I haven't decided my major yet." This was crazy. I was lying with too much ease. *Ugg!*

"Yeah, deciding a major can sometimes take a moment."

I desperately needed to get off the topic. "Where do you live?"

"I have my own spot in College Park, but I hang out here in Bankhead a lot because of school."

"You have a house there?"

"Well, it's an apartment, but hey, it's mine. And you?"

"Alpharetta. But I spend a lot of time with my grandmother in Bankhead though."

"Look at you, balling."

I laughed. "My parents are balling. I'm just along for the ride."

Ahmad cracked up. "I haven't laughed like this in a minute. You're cool. Not afraid to be yourself. I like that." He reached for my hand and his touch melted me.

A part of me felt like I needed to either tell him the truth or end the date and leave, but the bigger part of me wanted to stay and chill with him. And it had nothing to do with him being cute; it was more about the conversation and the way sitting here with him made me feel. So maybe . . . maybe . . . if I didn't lie about anything else . . . and prayed that I could remember the lies I'd already told, somehow we could chill and this would all be okay.

For the next two hours, Ahmad and I talked about everything under the sun. He was definitely special. "I enjoyed you tonight, ma," Ahmad said as he walked me to my car.

"Not as much as I enjoyed you." Now that was the truth. I blushed super hard. "Well, good night." I was unsure of whether I should kiss him or not.

"Good night," he said, and he must've read my mind, because as I turned away he pulled me back to him, softly pressed his lips against mine, and slid his heated tongue into my mouth. I think I saw stars . . . or maybe I touched the moon . . . or maybe the planets aligned . . . I'm not sure, but one thing I was certain of is that our kiss was the epitome of perfection.

The moment I stepped onto Nana's porch, the screen door flew open. "Chance!" Martini screamed and caused me to jump in fear.

My chest heaved up and down. "Are you crazy?" I blinked repeatedly. "You scared the heck out of me!"

"My fault, but I stayed behind and passed on hanging with the crew so that I could be here when you got back. So let's get to it, 'cause you took hella long on that date. I've been watching out the window for hours, waiting for you to come back. Now, I need to know what happened." She followed me to Keeya's room, where I kicked off my shoes and sat on the edge of the extra bed I claimed as my own on the weekends. "And don't front on the details either," she said. "Start from the beginning and end with the kiss."

I recapped the date for Martini and afterward I placed my hand over my heart and smiled. "I think I found the one." I fell back on the bed with the roses Ahmad had given me resting against my nose.

"Ahhh . . ." Martini fell beside me and slid one of the roses from my bouquet. She placed the rose on her chest and said, "I need you to hook me up with one of his friends."

7

Sittin' up in my room . . . thinkin' 'bout you . . .

—Brandy, "Sittin' Up in My Room"

It had been three hours, thirty-five minutes, and a few seconds that I'd been back at Nana's from my date with Ahmad, and no matter how I squeezed my eyes shut, tossed and turned in my bed, or internally screamed at myself to go to sleep . . . I couldn't.

But then again, I really didn't want to sleep. I wanted my mind to travel to the million places and worlds that my heart dreamed about. I felt like I could ballet dance on love taps, groove to my own music, be lost in my own zone. *Ugg! What the heck am I talking about? Have I turned into a crushin' poet? Don't look now, but I think I may need to be saved from myself.*

I settled deeper in my bed, pulled the sheet up to my chin, and turned over on my left side, then my right. I flipped onto my stomach, then onto my back, and after that I threw the towel in and sat up because I was about to lose it.

"Puhlease call, Ahmad. Puhlease," Martini growled and popped her lips as if they'd been stuck together. "'Cause all of that tossing and turning you're doing—"

"Is giving me the creeps," Keeya said as she pulled the covers from over her head.

"I thought it was just me." Ree-Ree ruffled her sleeping bag and fluffed her pillow. "Now call him so I can go back to sleep."

"If I call him, he's going to think I'm sweatin' him," I said.

"You are sweatin' him," Martini said.

"But I don't need him to know that."

"Umm-hmm, yeah you do." She carried on, "Ahmad sounds so fine that he should be in the needs-to-know-you-sweatin'-him category. It's okay, girl, 'cause you did better than me. I would've moved in with him already. I'm looking for an excuse to leave home."

"Leave home? Why?"

"'Cause Barbara be up in my B.I. just a lil too much. I be wanting to say, 'Mama, you need to step away from the business. I got this.'"

"You know Mama doesn't play that," Ree-Ree said. "So you may as well give it up."

"You're right, Ree-Ree. She doesn't. But ever since she drove us to the graveyard and showed us that double plot she bought for us—"

I blinked repeatedly. "She did what?"

"You heard me," Martini said. "She told us that if either one of us ever came at her out the side of our neck again, that's where we'd be living. So ever since then, I've been shook." She shuddered. "That's why I need me an escape route. Better known as a boo. You gon' hook me up with one of Ahmad's friends?"

"No," I said, not knowing whether I should laugh or ask Martini and Ree-Ree if their whole family was crazy. "I don't think that would be a good idea."

"Girl, don't play with me." She chuckled. "Now call that boy."

"Tonight was only their first date," Keeya said. "You should probably fall back a little."

"Fall back from what?" Martini frowned. "Chance, you only have three whole weeks left and then he expires. You better get your love grind on."

"Love? I just met him."

"And that's all the time you need," Martini insisted.

"What?"

"Look, all you need to fall in love is time enough to say, 'Hello, my name is Martini, I mean Chance, and I love you.' "

We all cracked up. "You need help," I said.

"And you need to call your man."

"Nah." I laid back down and settled my head into my pillow. "I'm cool."

"What . . . ever."

A half-hour later they snored and I stared at the ceiling. Umm, maybe I should, but then again . . . I looked at the clock: 1 A.M. Forget it. But . . . then . . . *I got it. I'll take the safe route. I'll text him.* I reached for my cell phone and texted: U Up? I pressed send and immediately after that I felt stupid.

I turned over and just as I'd kicked the butterflies out of my stomach, my phone beeped. He'd texted me back and immediately the butterflies moved back in. My eyes scanned his text. Call me.

WTH! OMG!

Clearly, I was trippin'. After a few seconds of lecturing myself that acting crazy wasn't healthy, I dialed Ahmad's number and he answered on the second ring.

"Wassup?" he said, and his voice sounded like sweet honey to my ears.

A million things to say raced through my mind, and then "I was thinking about you" slipped out. *That was so whack. I swear I needed more control over my emotions.*

I could hear him smiling. "Are you trying to set me up?"

"Set you up?" I was confused, yet teetering on feeling stupid.

"Yeah, set me up to telling you that I was lying here and thinking about you too?"

Really? "And what were you thinking?"

"About how much I really want to see you again."

Hey'yay! Don't look now, but I think I'm hot!
"Look at you, all up on me. Let me find out that
you have stalker qualities." *Screech! I don't be-*
lieve I said that. I may as well save myself from
further humiliation and hang up, 'cause I know
he thinks I'm dumb now.

He chuckled a little, but not enough for me to
judge whether or not he was amused or annoyed.

"I shouldn't have said that," I said quickly. "It's
just that—well—I didn't expect you to tell me you
were thinking about me too."

"Don't tell me you expected me to be like,
'Yeah, ma, I know you were thinking about me,
'cause what else is there for you to do?' "

"I didn't say all that now."

"Yes, you did, just not in those exact words.
The next time you call I'ma be like I see thoughts
of me are keeping you up all night again."

"Oh." I smiled. "You really riding yourself now.
I mean, you are cute and yeah, I was thinking
about you, but umm, you can calm down."

He chuckled. "Listen, ma," he said seriously.
"I'm diggin' you. You can take it, leave it, nurture
it, or simply see how it goes, but this is what I
need you to understand. I don't have a problem
being real about how I feel. Now, if that bothers
you, let me know and I'll hit you with a fist bump
and we'll keep it movin'."

I bit the corner of my lip. "I guess I'm not used
to . . . boys being . . . so upfront."

"Well, that's the difference between me and them."

"What's that?"

"I'm a man."

And that he was.

"Now," he continued, "the ball is in your court. We fist bumpin' or I'm picking you up tomorrow afternoon for dinner and a movie?"

Silence. Complete silence. Like, I didn't know what to say . . . and then I figured maybe I needed to stop thinking and just let things flow. So, I curled my knees to my chest and exhaled. "Movies. And I get to pick the movie."

Ahmad laughed. "No chick flicks."

"And what's a chick flick?"

"You know what a chick flick is."

"Are you talking about love stories?"

"Told you you knew what it was."

"I happen to like love stories!" I cracked up and before long I was nestled into bed with the phone to my ear, and for the rest of the night until the morning sun kissed the bedroom with rays of bright yellow light, I was lost in the best conversation I'd ever had in my life.

8

The sweetest thing I've ever known . . .

—LAURYN HILL, "THE SWEETEST THING"

"**C**hance!" Nana yelled down the hall and toward the bedroom, "There's a young man . . ." Her voice faded into the distance as she said, "What's your name, son?"

"Ahmad."

"Chance," she yelled again, "Ahmad is here to see you."

My heart thundered in my chest. What was he doing inside? I told him specifically to blow the horn for me. I broke out of the bedroom so fast that I'm sure I forgot something. But whatever. I had to get out of here before my grandmother ran her mouth and asked him a million questions. Nana's house was a small three-bedroom cape, but by the time I reached the living room, I was breathing as if I'd run through a mansion.

"Ahmad," I huffed, "what are you doing here?"

He and Nana looked at me like I had two heads. "What I meant was . . . umm, you didn't have to come in, Ahmad. You could've blown the horn."

Nana looked at me, perplexed. "That's rule number three." She twisted her lips. "If a young man comes here for one of my girls"—she turned toward Ahmad—"you ring the bell and make your presence known. Otherwise, you don't come here at all. Understood?"

"Yes, ma'am." He nodded.

She cut her eyes at me. "Got me?"

"Yes, Nana." I reached for my purse that was on the coffee table and placed it on my shoulder. "Are you ready, Ahmad?"

"Yeah." He smiled.

I kissed Nana on the cheek and said, "Bye, Nana."

"Chance," she whispered, "I think you might want to slip some shoes on."

I looked down at my bare feet and said, embarrassed, "Yeah, that would probably work. Ahmad, I'll meet you in the car, okay?"

"All right," he said. "Nice meeting you, Ms. Kennedy."

"You too, son." She smiled as he walked out of the house and the screen door closed behind him.

I hurried down the hall and slid on my Coach sneakers. After all, they complemented my fitted jeans and tee, and as I turned toward the bedroom door, Nana stood there.

"What is wrong with you?"

"Huh?" I laughed the fakest laugh in the world. "Nothing, Nana."

"Oh really?"

"Yeah, really."

"Umm-hmm, and how old is he?"

As I went to speak, my words crumbled in my mouth and the truth got lost on my tongue. "He's umm, eighteen."

"Eighteen?" She curled her lips.

"Yeah," I joked. "What? He looks thirty."

"He better not be thirty," she said seriously. "Now, is he thirty?"

"No." I scrunched my face.

"Chance, I let you have a lot of freedom, but don't push your luck. And I don't know why you're running around here acting like something is up, but you better speak now or forever hold your peace." She paused. " 'Cause if I find out you're lying to me, it won't be any peace."

Clearly, I had to get out of there. "Nana, it's cool. Trust me."

"Okay." She moved from the doorway. "Just remember what I said."

By the time I got into the car with Ahmad, I felt like I'd been to war and back. I really wanted to forget about my truth and live in the lie I'd created; it was much easier to deal with.

"Everything straight?" Ahmad said as he started to drive.

"Yeah," I assured him, "my grandmother's just overprotective."

HOT BOYZ

"I understand that. My mother's the same way. I have to say constantly, 'Ma, relax. I'm grown.' "

Wish I could say the same.

"Anyway,"—he draped his arm over the seat and instinctively I moved closer to him—"what are we going to see?"

"I want to go to the vintage theater downtown. They have a special showing of *Love Jones*."

He hesitated. "What? *Love Jones?* Didn't I tell you no chick flicks!" He stopped at a red light.

I laughed so hard tears fell from my eyes. "Ahmad, *Love Jones* is the bomb."

"Yeah, then you and your girls go and check it out. We're going to see an action movie."

"Action?"

"Chance, how am I going to explain to one of my boys that I went to the vintage theater to see *Love Jones?* Do you know how suspect that sounds?"

"It's not suspect, it's cute."

"You got me going to see a chick flick? And an old one at that. This is some bull ish."

I pushed my lips into a pout and Ahmad turned to me. His eyes clearly said he was on his way to giving in, so I pouted my lips even further to help my plight. "Come on," I said. "I promise you'll have a good time."

He stared at me, and then he moved in for a kiss. "Don't think I'ma be a sucker for you." He spoke against my lips.

"Don't worry. I won't let you be."

Ni-Ni Simone

* * *

"Admit it," I said as the movie ended and we rose from our seats. "You liked the movie. You were feeling the whole poetry vibe."

He slid his hands around my waist. "It was a'ight."

I slid my arms around his neck and looked into his eyes. For a moment I wondered: If I told him the truth would he continue to hold me or would he let me go . . . literally?

"What is it?" he said as if he could read my mind.

I sighed. "I just . . . I just . . ."

He peppered my lips with kisses. "Say it."

"I'm just having a good time with you."

"As long as you be yourself, we have a good time, and no matter what we always keep it one hundred, we can ride together forever."

"I would like that," I said as I placed my head against his chest and the movie's closing credits serenaded us. "I really would."

9

This lovin' I have . . .

—AALIYAH, "AGE AIN'T NOTHIN' BUT A NUMBER"

It had been the best month of my life. And never, ever, did I imagine having a cutie, well, a lil daddy, well, umm . . . scratch all of that because Ahmad was much more, he was a man. Sooo . . . never, ever did I imagine having a man, so sweet, and caring, with just the right dash of thug in him. It was like he had enough thug to check somebody, but it wasn't overdone where I'd be scared that he'd bust shots at any given moment. He was the type of guy I could bring home to my parents . . . and I wanted to bring him home to meet them . . . I just had to figure out a way to confess the truth. I mean, like sixteen was the age of consent, so it wouldn't really be that big of a deal if I told Ahmad how old I really was, right? After all, age was just a number . . . or was it more?

And besides, I was grown, right?

Yeah, I was grown.

So why did I feel frightened?

I turned over in bed and decided that I needed to tell Ahmad the truth. Like . . . I'd gone too far . . . I picked up the phone and started dialing Ahmad's number, yet before I completed the call, I heard someone saying, "Hello?"

"Hello?" I said, baffled.

"Wassup, ma?" It was Ahmad.

"Hey, I was just calling you," I said, doing my best to keep my mission in focus. "Listen, Ahmad—"

"I'm listening."

"This has been the best month ever and like . . . I want to be with you—"

He breathed a sigh of relief. "And I want to be with you too," he cut me off. "That's why I was calling you."

"But I have something to tell you." I swallowed.

"What's that?"

Ugg, I didn't even know where to start. "I'm just so . . . confused . . . and I'm not real sure what I'm feeling—"

"I felt the same way. I was confused too, at first, especially since it hasn't been that long that we've been kicking it and I didn't know how you would feel about this."

"Feel about what?"

"Feel about it being me and you . . . exclusively."

"You mean like be official? A couple?"

"Yeah. Like you should be my girl and I should be your man."

Tears filled my eyes; there was no way I could tell him anything that would spoil this moment. . . . "Yes," I said and dabbed the corners of my eyes. "Yes, I'll be your girl!"

"Now," he said and I could hear his smile, "there's only one thing I need you to do."

"What's that?"

"I want you to come outside."

I ran out of Keeya's bedroom, past a napping Nana in the living room and onto the porch. There he was. My man. My baby! I just wished guilt didn't rock the center of my chest the way it did. I needed to enjoy this moment without feeling like I had betrayed him. After all, I may have lied about my age, but everything I felt was real.

I ran straight into Ahmad's arms and hugged him tightly. "You know I would never do anything to intentionally hurt you," I said, pretty much out of nowhere.

"Where'd that come from?" he said, slightly confused, yet holding me closely. "Are you all right?"

"Yeah, I'm fine. I just never felt . . . anything like this."

"Me either." He kissed me softly on the lips.

"So I want you to wear this." He took his chain from around his neck and placed it around mine. "Hold this for me."

I smiled like crazy. "Are you sure?"

"Yeah, I'm sure." He gave me a soft peck. "Especially since I know that I have the hottest chick in the game wearing my chain."

I stood silent for a moment, and then Ahmad and I both cracked up laughing, "You already know how corny that was." I chuckled.

"I know it was corny, ma." He chuckled as he stroked my chin. "But it was the easiest way I knew that I could tell you I think I'm falling in love with you."

"You didn't tell me you were falling in love with me." I paused, and suddenly tears filled my eyes again. Don't look now, but I'm turning into a cry baby.

Ahmad pressed his forehead against mine and said, "Well, I'm telling you now."

Tears streaked my cheeks and Ahmad wiped them with the back of his thumb. "I'm falling in love with you too," I said as I laid my head against his chest. "Really, really falling in love with you."

10

Shawty, you can't handle this . . .

—Xscape, "Wassup"

"Now, look. If either of you two can't Roller-blade, let us know now," I said to Ahmad and his friend, Jarrett, who sat next to Martini in the backseat. I hoped like heck that Martini and Jarrett really liked each other, because it took me a minute to comb through Ahmad's friends and find one who I felt was right for my girl. But once I found the tall and mocha-colored Jarrett, I knew he was the one. He went to school with Ahmad and was also from Harlem.

We'd arranged their first meeting as a double date with us and so far they'd hit it off pretty well.

We were in Ahmad's kitted-up and pearlized black Honda Accord, when we pulled into Stone Mountain's skating rink.

"Now don't front," Martini said to the guys,

"'cause we don't want to be embarrassed on the floor."

"Who are they talking to?" Ahmad looked at Jarrett in the rearview mirror.

Jarrett shrugged his shoulders. "I know they don't call themselves playing the New York boyz."

"Nah, that can't be it," Ahmad said. " 'Cause in Harlem we skate all day every day. So if anything we need to be worried about you two." Ahmad got out the car, walked around, and opened my door. "Now, don't break the cardinal rule and fall. Please"—his eyes roamed all over me—"and don't be pulling on me either."

"Boy, please." I pressed my lips against his. "I can skate better than you!"

"Is that a challenge?" He kissed me back.

"It can be. What, you got money to blow?" I slid my arms around his neck.

"Twenty bills."

"Twenty bills." I kissed him and then whispered against his lips, "And when I beat you, don't cry either." I gave him one last peck.

"Did you two forget this is a G-rated double date?" Martini asked. "I'm just sayin'."

"Don't hate, Martini," I said as we started to walk. "Don't hate."

"Ain't no party like a skate party!" the DJ yelled as we walked in the door. We rented a small personal locker, where we all placed our shoes and locked them away. Afterward we took a seat and slid on our blades. Mine were hot pink with rhinestones across the toe and of course Martini's were zebra. Ahmad and Jarrett's blades were sleek black.

The only light in the place came from the DJ booth and a spinning disco ball that twirled around in the center of the rink and reflected a sea of primary colors. The music was definitely underground with a hot base line that lured everybody to the floor and forced them to dance.

Martini and I bladed backwards into the center of the rink. We motioned our index fingers for Ahmad and Jarrett to join us on the floor. "Come on, baby." I dropped down to the floor and popped back up. "You got to get it how you live and it's time to get poppin'!"

As if on cue the DJ dropped Xscape's classic "What's Up" and that was all Martini and I needed to take this to another level. We broke out into our Thick-n-Juicy routine that we usually did when we hit the rink on Sundays, but being that we were here with two cuties, we dropped it on 'em real quick and by the time we were done all they could do was stand back, reach in their pockets, and hand us each twenty-dollar bills.

"Told you," Martini said as she skated in her spot.

"Yup-yup." I smiled and slid my money in my pocket.

We were having the time of our lives and I couldn't imagine it getting any better than this, which is why when we sat in the food court I was caught totally off guard when Jarrett asked Martini when she'd be nineteen and she said, "Right after I turn eighteen."

"Martini, stop playing." I laughed and lied all in the same breath. "You better stop teasing Jarrett like that. Her birthday is in January."

Martini looked at me as if I had lost every bit of my mind, and then she said, "Umm-hmm, whatever she said."

"What do you mean?" Jarrett asked. "You don't know when your birthday is?" He looked puzzled.

"Of course I do." Martini smiled and waved her hand. "You know I like to be funny every now and then." She chuckled. "I'll be back; I have to go to the bathroom."

"I'll join you." I smiled.

We waved at the boys as we walked away from the table. Once we reached the bathroom door, we pushed it open and Martini snapped, "Chance, what the heck is going on?! I hope you don't have me involved in no illegal activity. Oh, Lawd." She started to cry. "The graveyard. Oh, Lawd, the graveyard! My mama is gon' kill me. They gon' change my name to Rest In Peace, 'cause Barbara is gon' beat my—"

"Martini!" I yelled, shaking her by the shoulders. "Would you get it together? It's nothing like that."

Her face looked as if she were returning from out of space. "Then what is it?"

"Ahmad—"

"What, did he do something? Is he a criminal? Don't tell me he's on the run? Why do they always come to Atlanta—?"

"Martini—"

"Look, I can't end up on the news, because my uncle, who just moved in with us, has a mouth full of gold-encrusted teeth, a long Jheri curl, and a southern drawl that sounds like it comes from the bottom of his feet. So trust me, we don't want him doing a commentary! Trust."

"It's nothing that would land us on the news."

"Then what is it? Don't tell me he has some baby mamas you didn't know about."

"No, no baby mamas—"

"Don't tell me he had some stank-behind disease." She popped her lips.

"No, that wasn't—"

"Oh no, is he on the down low? You know that's another thing Atlanta is known for, 'cause my cousin—"

"Martini, do you want me to tell you the real story? Or do you want to make up your own version?" I snapped.

"Pause." She had the nerve to sound offended. "You can calm down."

"Look, I lied to Ahmad and told him I was eighteen."

"Okay, we can fix that."

"How?"

"Go out there and tell him you forgot to tell him you are really sixteen. That you were on medication that day and you're just realizing what you said."

I couldn't believe she said that. "That makes . . . absolutely . . . no sense!"

"Neither did telling the man of your dreams that you were eighteen!"

"Look, I need to know what to do."

Martini thought for a moment and then she asked, "How old is he?"

"Twenty-two."

"What?!" she screamed. "Dang, girl, it's a good thing you turned sixteen or he'd have a problem, 'cause it would be clink-clink and lights out." She curled her upper lip. "Do you realize he's old enough to be your granddaddy? All right now, dirty old men in the hizouse!"

"Would you be serious! See, I knew I shouldn't have said anything to you. Forget it, I'll figure it out on my own."

"Listen," Martini said, "I don't know what you trippin' for. Seriously, age is only a number."

"What?" I said, stunned. "But Martini, how do I clean up a lie like that?"

"Look, Chance, you take things to the extreme. You act like you're about to marry this cat. Just have fun. You know my motto: free meals, movies, and dates. Then the month is up and we rotate. Hey'yay! And he's about a half-hour overdue to be dumped. Soooo after we leave here, can him. You're due for a new lil daddy anyway. No need of holding on to him all summer. How played is that?"

"I love him. I don't want to let him go."

"Well, hmph, yeah"—she nodded—"you got a problem. But then again, don't sweat it. Skip all the worry and just go with the flow. Like my mama says, if you think bad things, bad things will come to you. So think happy and fun times and that's what you'll have."

I'm not convinced that anything she had to say made sense. All I knew was that I wanted it to make sense because in some twisted sort of way, it made me feel better. "True," I agreed. "Maybe you're right, Martini."

"I know I am. Now, let's go back out there and beat them out of the rest of their dollars. Hmph, 'cause Martini Alizé Sherell needs a new pair of shoes, honey!"

11

I'd been with Ahmad every day for half of the summer and I'd told more lies than I could remember. I never expected to really fall for Ahmad or be caught up in a beautiful moment every time we were together. I felt like . . . like a queen or maybe a celebrity when I was wrapped in his arms. And every time I laid my head against his chest, I remembered the lies that lay between us, which forced me to end the date, and have guilt drag me home.

Sweat dampened my brow as I tossed and turned in bed and attempted to settle by lying on my back. I stared at the glow in the dark stars Keeya had on her ceiling. But after a few minutes of wondering why a powder-pink room had a navy-blue ceiling with illuminated stars and gray-ish clouds, I knew this wasn't the position for me either, so I sat up, and of course visions of Ahmad danced before my eyes.

"Keeya," I said in a soft, hissing whisper, "you up?" When she didn't answer I called her again. "Keeya, Keeya . . . Keeya."

"Huh?" she said groggily. "Mama, I promise I won't forget to wash the dishes again. Just let me sleep for five more minutes, please."

What? "Keeya, I am not your mama."

She hesitated. "Then you don't need to be waking me up!" She turned over and settled even deeper into the bed.

"Keeya, could you wake up for a moment please?"

"OMG! This better be good." She lay on her back and faced the ceiling.

"That's okay. Never mind," I said. "If you're tired, you can go back to sleep."

"What?" She smacked her lips, and said groggily, "You woke me up out of my beauty sleep at three o'clock in the morning to tell me never mind? Chance, if you don't tell me something it will be a situation."

"No," I said somberly, "I don't want to bother you."

"You know what," she snapped, "if I get up from here I'm coming for your throat."

"Why are you so violent? Maybe you need to see somebody about that."

"Nawl, hell nawl," Keeya said in a heavy southern drawl, "I'm dreamin' and this here moment doesn't exist." She turned over on her side, settled her head into her pillow and a few seconds later she was snoring.

I hated to wake her up again, but I had to. "Keeya."

"Okay, Chance," she said, a little too calm. "If you don't tell me something this time"—she pounded her fist on the nightstand—"I got a trick for you."

I sighed. "All right, you know . . . like . . . me and Ahmad have been going out for over a month now."

"And?"

"Like, I really feel a connection with him that I've never felt with anyone."

"Sooooo, are you in love with him?"

"Yes."

"Have you told him that?"

"Yes."

"Great, way to go." She turned back over. "Good night."

"It's more than that though."

"More than what?" She turned back to face me.

"I've been . . ." I paused. "Well, I've been lying to him."

"Why?" I could hear the frown in her voice. "What would you be lying about?"

"My age. He thinks I'm eighteen."

"What?" She flicked on the lamp that sat on the

nightstand, causing the stars to stop glowing and instead a dull yellow strip of light to slide down the center of the room. "What do you mean he thinks you're eighteen?"

"Well . . . you know when we were in Club Abyss that night, everybody knows you have to be twenty-one and over."

"So why didn't you tell him the truth?"

"I can't."

"Why?"

"Because he's much older than me."

"And how old is that?"

"Well, you know if he was in Club Abyss he has to be over twenty-one."

"Why are you talking in circles? This is really pissing me off! We were in Club Abyss and we are nowhere near twenty-one, so no, just because he was in there didn't make him over twenty-one! Now, I'ma ask you this one last time! How old is he?"

"Twenty-two."

"Have you lost your mind?! He's thirty-two—?"

"I said twenty-two!"

"He's old as heck!"

"Are you hearing me? And besides, how old did you think he was? You knew he was grown!"

"Puhlease, I knew he was cute! I never thought about how grown he was. So when are you breaking things off with him?"

"Breaking it off? I can't . . . ummm . . . I don't think I want to do that."

"Then you need to tell him the truth!"

"So he can think I'ma liar?"

"You *are* lying to him!"

"If he knew I was sixteen he would stop seeing me!"

"And that's what he should do. That's a grown man! If he gets caught up messing with you, do you know the trouble he would get into?"

"No, sixteen is the age of consent!"

"And I'm sure you've said that to everybody who'll listen, but it's not going to fly with me. What you're doing isn't right."

"I didn't say that."

"Then what are you saying?"

"I love him!"

"Girl, please. Stop being so selfish and dead that relationship. Because you know if your parents find out, Moms-zilla will serve him right!"

Silence. This wasn't the reaction I expected. Keeya and I usually agreed on everything, but this threw a monkey wrench in it. "What if"—I sighed— "I can keep the relationship going, but keep it a secret from everybody except you? And then when I'm in my twenties and it's time for us to get married, I tell him and everybody else the truth."

Keeya blinked and then she stared at me as if I'd lost my mind. She flicked the light off and turned over in bed. "You're officially stupid," she said. "Dead it."

I swallowed hard. I hated that she was right.

And I hated that the love between Ahmad and me was right, but the circumstances were all wrong.

Ahmad's chain felt cold against my neck and tears filled the corners of my eyes. I had to end it. Dead it. And move on. I would never forget him, but I had to drop him.

12

Just can't leave you alone . . .

—Ciara, "Can't Leave 'Em Alone"

"**D**eecceevaaaas!" Martini snapped her fingers. "I just want y'all to know that after I broke up with Hakeem, and then Farad—oh yeah, and I dumped Jarrett, last week"—she glanced over at me—"I have met Mr. August: Elliot Jones. And he's so fine; he just might make his way through September too."

"Mr. August?" I frowned. "Elliot? Who is that? And why did you break up with Jarrett?"

"Because," Martini said, "the month was up and it was time to go from the ex-boo to the next boo."

"But you just met Jarrett," I said.

"Listen, how many times have I told you, that after a month has passed that you're supposed to dump your boo at the height of relationship? Why do you keep holding on?"

"Because I like my boyfriends for longer than a month!"

"Well, that's a mess, honey. I was with Hakeem, one week, two days, five hours, and twenty-six minutes past his expiration date, and you see what happened to me!"

"But that had nothing to do with the length of time," Keeya said.

"Girl, bye," Martini said. "You sound real crazy."

"Is anybody else confused?" Ree-Ree asked. "Why do you have a month's time limit on your boyfriends?"

"Duh!" Martini snarled. "It'll make them remember me and if I ever want to go back to them, I can."

"And how is that?" Ree-Ree asked.

"I can't believe we're sisters." Martini smacked her lips. "No matter how I try and school you, we are nothing alike. Now look, if you dump them right after a hot date or after he's confessed his love, then he'll always wonder what the relationship could've been." Martini rolled her eyes to the ceiling. "Do I have to school you three on everything?"

"I don't believe you, Martini." I shook my head. "I will not be introducing you to anybody else."

"Don't get mad, diva. Just don't introduce me to somebody new on or around the fifteenth and then they can get a whole month."

"Shaking my head," Ree-Ree said.

"Anywho, now, let me tell y'all about Elliot,"

Martini carried on. "Deeeeevaaas, he is so fine. But the only problem is that he has three baby mamas."

"How old is he?" Keeya frowned.

"Seventeen."

"Yuck." Ree-Ree curled her upper lip.

"Imagine how I felt," Martini said.

"How'd you find out?" Keeya asked. "He told you?"

"No, I broke into his Facebook account and he had three messages with the subjects of Baby Mamas, 1, 2, and 3. So after I saw that mess, I turned around and broke into his Twitter account and sure enough, they were following him."

"You did what!" Ree-Ree said, surprised.

"Broke into his Facebook and Twitter!" Martini said, proud of herself. "Why? What's the problem?"

Keeya snapped, "Why do you have to be reminded of Thick-n-Juicy's constitution all the time?" Keeya opened her nightstand drawer and ruffled the constitution in Martini's face. "It clearly states that if you have to be jacking your man's e-mail, Facebook, MySpace, Twitter, Skype, or even his car, it's time to say bye-bye because you have now become a what?"

"A stalker," Ree-Ree answered.

"Whatever." Martini flicked her hand and lay back on the bed. "Whatever. He's cute and he'll do for the month and that's all that matters."

"That's a hot mess," I said dryly while looking

at the clock: 9 P.M. I was seriously irked and there was no way I could continue to listen to this. What I really wanted to do was kick it with my baby, Ahmad. I'd been sending him to voice mail, not returning any of his calls, and avoiding him like the plague all week—all behind feeling unsure—and talking to Keeya didn't help things at all. And now I felt horrible. I wanted Ahmad back. Period. And I'd figure out how to come clean later.

"Chance!" Ree-Ree snapped her fingers. "Earth to Chance."

"Yeah, yeah," I said, uncertain of how long they'd been calling me. "What? What is it?"

"Do you wanna go skating?"

I hesitated, and as tempting as it was I shrugged my shoulders and said, "No. Not really."

Martini blinked in disbelief. "No? You don't wanna go and drop it on these fools? Can't nobody pop it on Rollerblades like our crew, and you don't wanna go? Really?"

"Nope," I said with little to no conviction. "I just umm . . . I'ma get going."

"Why are you leaving so early?" Keeya asked.

"I don't feel too good. I might come back later on, though." I stood up and grabbed my purse and overnight bag.

"Okay," Martini said, "but I'ma walk you to the door."

"All right. Bye, Keeya," I said. "Bye, Ree-Ree."

"See you later." They waved, as I walked out

the room with Martini a short distance behind me.

Once we stood on the porch and the screen door closed behind us, Martini asked me, "Wassup? What's wrong with you?"

"Nothing's wrong."

Martini twisted her lips. "Now we lying to each other? You know I know you. We tight like barbecue flavor on pork rinds, so stop the madness and tell me what's the deal with you? Something happened between you and Ahmad?"

I sighed. "Yeah," I said with a drag. "I've been avoiding him all week. I haven't returned his calls, haven't answered my phone. This whole thing just sucks!"

"Why did you do that?" Her eyes grew big. "He really loved you and you've been seeing him all summer—the one-month rule no longer applied. You shouldn't have dumped him."

"It had nothing to do with the one-month rule."

"Then what? What happened?"

"This whole lying to him every time I saw him. Like it really started to get to me. And plus I told Keeya and she freaked out on me. It was just too much. Really it was."

"First of all, you know Keeya can be a little judgmental at times, so you have to take her advice with a grain of salt."

"True."

"And nobody has really seen you two together

like me, and I know you love him and I know he loves you."

"I do love him."

"Well, that's real. So what lies are you talking about? Your age? Please. When the time is right, you'll tell him, but until then I wouldn't say a word. Now if you don't slip up and invite him to the prom you'll be cool, for at least another year."

"I don't know about that, Martini."

"Psst, puhlease, I would keep it movin'. Besides, if you break it down, you two are closer in age than you think."

I looked at her, puzzled. "And how is that?"

"Listen, girls mature faster than boys, so really he's like four years younger than his age."

"Four years?"

"Four years. So that makes him what? Eighteen," she said.

"Eighteen?"

"Boom, there it is. Sixteen and eighteen, perfect together." She clapped her hands. "Now go get your man, girl."

"Nah," I said, "I'm going home."

I'd been on the highway for about five minutes when my car made a strange sound and slowed down. My heart jumped around in my chest. I was in the middle lane and if I didn't pull over quickly, it wouldn't be pretty. I was able to inch over to the right shoulder and just as I was about to put my car in park it died.

OMG!

What the heck just happened? Cars flew past me and police were nowhere in sight. I had to call my father, so I pulled out my cell phone and dialed his number quickly only for no one to pick up. *Maybe he didn't hear the phone ring.* I dialed his number again and nothing.

I called my mother and no one answered her line either. I promise you I wanted to scream. Here I was stuck on the highway and my parents were too busy doing their own thing to even answer the phone for me. Damn! I was certifiably pissed, and I couldn't call Nana, because Nana didn't drive.

Ahmad . . . but no, I can't call him for a favor when I've been playing him all week. But I can't stay here. . . . Know what, I'ma call him real quick, tell him what I need, and if he acts funny, I'll hang up. I dialed his number, but my nerves forced me to hang up after the first ring. *Okay . . . okay . . . okay . . . this is stupid! Utterly stupid! I can not sit on this highway like this. I should call the police . . . but then again . . . Ahmad said he was good with cars . . . so maybe . . . maybe he'll help me. . . . Yeah, that's it, he'll help me.*

I dialed Ahmad's number and this time I let the phone ring until he answered. "Hello?"

"Ahmad, hey," I said nervously. "Wassup? How are you?"

"I'm good."

"Oh, that's cute," I said, sounding real dumb. "I was just calling to see how you were."

"Okay, cool. I'm straight. Now that we've squared that, I'ma let you go. One." Click.

"Hello?" *Did he just hang up on me? Forget it, I'm not about to sweat him.* I called my parents again, only to go through another round of unanswered calls, which meant I had to call Ahmad back.

I dialed his number and prayed that he answered, and when he did, I suddenly became speechless. "Hello?" he said.

"Ummm, yeah, Ahmad, I umm . . ." Why were the words dripping slowly out of my mouth?

"Chance, are you all right?"

I sighed deeply. "Look, I know you're probably pissed with me right now, being that I've been acting shady all week, but I promise you I have a good explanation for that . . . which I really can't explain right now," I said without taking a breath, "because I'm out here on I-85 and my car has died. I don't know what's wrong with it and I can't get my mother or father on the phone . . . so . . ."

"You need me to be Superman, again," he said, clearly pissed off.

"Ahmad, listen, I didn't mean to—"

"Look," he said with a serious attitude, "skip all of that. Really, I'm not beat for it. Now, I'ma come and get you, but make this the last time you expect me to come and save you, 'cause that's not my plight. A'ight." And he hung up.

I wanted to be mad, but I couldn't stop smiling and ten minutes later when I saw Ahmad's headlights pull up behind me and he got out the car, holding a flashlight in his hand, I was about to burst. I wanted to run out the car and hug him, but judging by the look on his face, he wasn't in the mood. "Pop the hood," he said sternly, as he walked around the passenger side of the car to the front.

I popped the hood and he said, "Turn the ignition."

I did and nothing.

"Beep the horn."

The horn worked.

"Flash the lights."

The lights flashed.

"Turn the ignition again."

Nothing.

"A'ight." He slammed the hood and walked over to the passenger window. "You need a new transmission. Call AAA, have them tow the car and they'll take you home."

I couldn't believe this. "Call a triple who?"

He shook his head. "Call a tow truck."

"Okay, okay, that's a good idea." I scrolled through the yellow pages in my iPhone, found a local towing service, and dialed the number. I gave them my name and information. "Thank you, ma'am," the operator said. "We'll be there, but it will take a few hours."

"What do you mean a few hours?" I asked in a panic. "How many hours is that?"

"I'm not sure, three, maybe four. There's a major collision on the other highway and all of our trucks are out right now, but as soon as one comes back in, we'll be there."

OMG. "Okay," I said with a slight edge to my voice, "fine." I hung up and looked at Ahmad. "It's going to take about three or four hours."

"Cool, well, at least you know they're coming." He turned away. "Keep your doors locked."

"Keep my doors locked?" I said in disbelief. "So you just gon' leave me?"

"Nah. I'ma get in my car, wait for the tow truck to get here and then I'm out."

"I just said that would take hours. I don't want to be here for hours."

"It's not always about what you want. Sometimes it's about what somebody else wants. But you wouldn't know that because you're too selfish to realize that!"

"I'm not selfish!" I screamed.

"Then where the hell have you been?" he snapped. "I been calling you all week, nonstop, sweatin' you, and I don't sweat anybody. But here, I've been sweatin' you. Nah, that won't work. But it's cool, because this whole deal with you is a wrap."

"So what are you saying?"

"I've said it. I'm done. So do you and I'ma do me!"

My heart cracked in two and the fragments filled my throat. I didn't expect this and now I knew this is not what I wanted. I wanted my relationship back. I wanted to get things back to where they needed to be and everything else could be figured out and put together later, but right now it was about winning my man back.

I hurried out the car and over to Ahmad. "I'm sorry," I said to him. "I've just been . . . confused."

"Save the confusion. It's cool. Now get back in the car and wait for the tow truck."

"But that's not what I want to do."

"So what you wanna do?"

"I wanna go home with you."

I could tell by the way he paused that I caught him off guard. "I don't think that's a good idea."

"Why?"

"Because of everything I just told you. You play too many games and at the very moment I thought you were different, you showed me your hand. So I'm good."

"Ahmad, it wasn't like that."

"Like what, like what I thought you were? Yeah, you got a few dates out of me, but it's cool. And now that you've shown me that you're not feeling me—"

"What are you talking about?!" I said. "I'm more than feeling you—"

"I can't tell!"

"I love you."

"Love is more than words."

I didn't know exactly how to respond to that, so I said, "Ahmad, I've been going through some things lately and I don't know what to do."

"You're supposed to come to me. I'm your man! That's what I'm here for."

"Yeah, but I don't want you to think I'm crazy or nuts because I'm going through changes."

"Chance, we're both going through things, but as long as we have each other, that's all that matters."

"I just thought—"

"You think too much. A relationship is give and take. When something is bothering you, you're supposed to turn to me, not away from me."

"You're right. So what happens now?"

"I love you, Chance, but I can't go through this every time you're feeling a certain way."

"This won't happen again. I promise." I pressed my lips against his.

"A relationship," he said, "is about being able to be up front with each other. Being able to tell one another, that I've never felt like this—" And before he could finish we kissed. "You still wanna go home with me?" he asked, sliding kisses over my neck.

"Yeah," I said, tossing caution to the wind. "Yeah, that's exactly what I want to do."

13

No regrets, just love . . .

—KATY PERRY, "TEENAGE DREAM"

"Psst, Ahmad—Ahmad . . ." I lured him out of his sleep and "Wake up" forced his eyes to open. I laid next to him and softly stroked his arm. He turned toward me and wiped the cold out of his eyes. "Sorry to wake you up so early," I said. "But listen, I need you to take me home."

"Take you home?" He looked at the clock, which read 9 A.M.

"Take me home." I hopped out the bed and began to frantically dress. There was no way I was supposed to be here all night. I had to get out of here before my mother overreacted and there was an APB out for me. The plan was to come and chill with Ahmad for a few hours, make up, and then have him drop me off at Nana's. Not spend the night with him. Not wake up next to him, like this was really cool. I had to go home, and quickly.

"You want to go home now?" He looked bewildered.

"Right now." I grabbed my purse for confirmation. The last thing I needed was for my entire day to be a problem. Maybe I needed to see how many calls I'd missed. Yeah, that's it. That way I'd know how many stories I needed to come up with. I sorted frantically through my purse.

"What's wrong with you?" Ahmad sat up in bed. "Did I miss something?"

"No . . ." I said distantly as I continued to sort through my purse, only to come up with nothing. "Freak!" I gritted my teeth as my heart zoomed past my stomach and headed straight for my feet. *Think . . . think . . . think . . .* What was I going to say when I made it home? My parents were a lot of things, but dumb wasn't one of them. And yeah, Nana was the coolest grandmother in the world. She let us party, hang out until a reasonable hour, and she never ever got in our way. But if we ever broke one of the two rules—well, three rules— she had, she flipped her wig; and that was fa'sho. The last time Keeya called herself sneaking out and then creeping back in the house in the wee hours of the morning, Nana padlocked her room, made her delete all two thousand of her friends on Facebook, shut down her Twitter account, and made her sign in and out every time she left the house. Can you say hell knows no fury like a grandmama scorned? So, imagine what Nana would do to me? Especially knowing she'd already warned me.

Think . . . think . . . think . . . I was completely messed up in the game and all I could see headed for me was a tsunami.

I needed Jesus.

"Chance," Ahmad said with an edge to his voice, "do you hear me? What's the problem? It's obvious that something is wrong."

"Look"—I hesitated—"I . . . umm . . . promised my mother that I would help her set up . . . for ummm . . . a yard sale—"

"A yard sale?" he questioned.

"I know," I said as I slipped my shoes on. "Long story. But please, I really need you to take me home. Okay?"

"A'ight." He got out of bed and started to dress. "And you're sure everything is fine?"

Oh my God, if he asks me that one more time! "Ahmad, it's cool."

As he continued to dress, I paced the room, trying to think of what I could say. What excuse I could use. *Martini. That's it! I'll use Ahmad's phone, call and leave a voice mail message on my mother's phone and say that I stayed the night with Martini. Yeah, I got it! And I'll soften it with an apology. . . . Oh God, she'll never believe that. Yeah, that's it—they picked me up, it was late and I didn't want to wake Nana. Boom! There it is.*

"Chance—"

"What?!" I snapped.

"Look, what the heck is wrong with you? And don't lie."

"I'm cool. I told you I have to help my mother with a cleaning out the garage."

"You said a yard sale."

"Same difference."

"No." He grabbed his car keys. "That's a different lie."

"Ahmad"—I reached for his hand—"it's nothing." I shrugged my shoulders, as an attempt to play things off. "I just don't want my mother to get worried about me. That's all. I know she was expecting me a while ago."

"Why don't you use my phone and call her?" he said as we walked out of the apartment and got into his car.

"No, it's okay. I'll explain it to her when I get there."

"So you want me to drop you off in Alpharetta." He started to drive.

"Hell no—" I stammered. "I mean, no, no. Drop me off in Bankhead."

"Your mother must really be something," he said as we walked out of his apartment.

"Yeah, she is." I laughed and he laughed, but both laughs sounded phony.

"Well." He smiled. "You're allowed one pass. Your mother will understand."

"Yeah, one pass and then they kill me." I tried

to act as if I was laughing because what I said was funny, but I was laughing because I was nervous and there was nothing else to do with all of this anxious energy. "Maybe the next time I come over, I won't need to leave in such a hurry and we'll get to kick it." I looked at Ahmad and gave him as genuine of a smile that I could muster.

"Yeah, maybe," he said. "I hate that our day has to get started like this though."

"Me too, but I really need to check on my car."

"Your car?"

"Yeah, my car. Yard sale, clean up, go grocery shopping, it's a whole laundry list of things I need to do."

"You sure you don't want to use my phone to call your mom and tell her where you are at least?"

"Ahmad." I did my best to keep my voice steady. "Trust me. It's best if I don't do that. Maybe we can hook up later on today. After I shower . . . and umm . . ." *After I tell some lies and figure out a way to clean up this mess I've made.* "I'll get dressed. Yeah, get dressed and we can chill."

Ahmad turned onto my grandmother's street and there were three cop cars with sirens blaring in front of her house. And haphazardly parked in front of the cop cars were my parents' vehicles.

Dead.

Flat line . . .

"Look"—I turned to Ahmad—"drop me off, right here. Okay?"

"On the corner?" He frowned. "I'm not drop-

ping you off on the corner and especially with these cop cars out here like that. Anything could
happen to you and apparently they must be looking for somebody."

Yeah, me. "Ahmad, really, you need to drop me off. Don't even stop the car, just slow down enough for me to roll out, and keep going. Trust me."

"What kinda . . . ? Chance, I'm not doing that. Nothing's that bad." He rode past the corner and pulled in front of Nana's house and placed the gear in park.

And just as I went to hurry out of the car and yell, "Step on the gas and go!" three police officers walked swiftly to the car and my mother burst through the door screaming, "There she is!" And before I could say anything, one cop had yanked my door and the others were snatching Ahmad out the car and slapping handcuffs on him.

"What are you doing?" I screamed. "Let him go!"

"You mean to tell me that this is what you've been doing?" my mother yelled at me with my father standing by her side. Nana, Keeya, Martini, and Ree-Ree were standing there too. "Letting this thirty-two-year-old man take advantage of you? And don't lie either, because Keeya told us everything."

I looked at Keeya as if she'd lost her mind, but before I could say anything she said, "We were worried about you! I couldn't keep that a secret!"

"A thirty-two-year-old man, Chance!" Nana said.

"And I asked you how old he was and you lied to me! Why would you do something like this?"

"What the hell is going on?!" Ahmad yelled. "Chance." He looked at me. "What's going on? Why are they arresting me?"

"You have the right to remain silent . . ." the arresting officer said as he read Ahmad his Miranda rights.

My head was seconds from splitting open. This felt like a dream, but I knew I was walking in reality. Tears streamed down my face as the officers patted Ahmad down and removed his wallet from his back pocket.

"Why are you arresting him?" I screamed.

"Where have you been, Chance?" my mother screamed.

"I didn't do anything!" Ahmad yelled.

"Why are you having him arrested!" I screamed at the top of my lungs. "He didn't do anything! He didn't know I was sixteen!"

"Sixteen?" Ahmad looked at me and his eyes became glassy. "You've been lying to me all this time? Do you realize I could lose everything?"

"Oh, you will lose everything," my mother promised. "I'ma see to that!"

"Where were you, Chance?" my father interjected. "You had us worried sick about you."

"I'm fine. Okay," I said as tears rolled down my face and snot slid from my nose. "Please let him go. He didn't know." My voice cracked as my words muddled by tears. "He didn't know. . . ." The officers walked Ahmad to their car and pushed him into the backseat. "Where are they taking him?"

"To jail. And by the time I'm done prosecuting him, he'll be under the jail"—my mother looked at one of the officers—"for child endangerment, and whatever other charges fit."

"Would you listen to me?" I ran behind the officer walking Ahmad to the car, and as I went to grab the officer by the arm, another grabbed me and pulled me back.

"He didn't know." I cried like a baby. "He didn't know." I turned to my father. "Daddy, please listen to me—"

"No, Chance, that's the problem. I've listened to you a little too much—"

"You haven't listened to me at all! You never listen to me! Everything is always about you and you!" I pointed to my mother. "You never hear me!"

"I don't want to hear it!" my father snapped. "We've been worried sick about you—"

"And here I had to miss work!" my mother spat.

I can't believe she said that. "Everything is work, work, work!" I yelled. "This is about his life!"

"Watch your tone!" my father said. "I don't know what has gotten into you!"

"Bad parenting," Nana said, "that's what's gotten into her. I've been telling you two for years that there's more to being a parent than buying everything a child wants. This girl needs parents, not sponsors. She needs your attention and maybe if you'd been giving her the attention she's been craving, then she wouldn't be tied up with this old scum bag!" Nana turned to me. "Now, what you did was wrong, but I'm not convinced that your parents didn't push you there. What would make you think you could leave your car on the side of the road and we wouldn't panic?"

"The car broke down and I had the car towed," I said in a panic. "I tried to call my parents and they never answered the phone, but I called Ahmad and he came to get me!"

"I bet he did," my mother snapped. "And you need to stop lying because the car was never towed. The police found it on the side of the road. Abandoned! With your cell phone in it!"

"What?!"

"Yes." Tears rattled my mother's voice. "And I know I may not be the best mother, but you have no idea! Do you know what went through my mind when the police showed up at my door and you were nowhere to be found?"

"Ma, listen to me. I have been trying to get your attention and daddy's attention for I don't know how long—all of my life—and all you ever did was work. I'm not saying what I did was right, but Ahmad was there for me. He loved me and he trusted me. He is not my problem, I'm his, and please, I have to fix this. Please, please. Let him go."

My mother stared at me for what felt like forever, and then she said quietly, but loud enough for the officers to hear her, "Let him go."

"Let him go?" my father asked, surprised.

"Are you sure, D.A.?" one of the officers asked, calling my mother by her title.

"Yeah." She swallowed. "He's not the problem."

The officer helped Ahmad out of the car and uncuffed him. I could tell that Ahmad was beyond hurt and there was nothing I could do or knew how to do, to change this moment and make it disappear.

I wanted to run over to Ahmad as he walked back to his car and tell him that the only lie between us was my age. I loved him and I wanted to love him forever . . . all I needed was for him to forgive me.

"Ahmad," his name slipped from between my lips, but he didn't look my way. Instead, he got into his car and took off, leaving nothing but his memory behind.

I knew at any moment I was going to break into pieces. I just didn't know who would catch me, and unexpectedly my mother wrapped her arms around me and said, "I'm sorry."

"He didn't know."

"I believe you." She stroked my hair. "I believe you."

"See, I knew it," I heard Martini whisper behind me. "Had she stuck to my one-month rule, *Law & Order* wouldn't be rollin' out in the streets."

14

I'll see you next lifetime . . . no hard feelings . . .

—ERYKAH BADU, "NEXT LIFETIME"

A year later . . .

"**M**a!" I yelled from my room. "Can you come here?!"

"What is it, Chance?" my mother said as her slippers slapped their way down the hall. "I'm trying to help your dad unpack his things. You know he's been taking a piece here and a piece there out of his suitcases since he's moved back home."

"I know, Ma, but can you please explain to Martini that she can not wear a size five, because she doesn't seem to listen to us."

My mother looked Martini over and smiled. "You know I love myself some, Martini," she said, "and I think she looks cute. Work it, gurl." She snapped her fingers.

All I could do was laugh. My mother had become someone completely different from who she was before. She wasn't so rigid. She listened.

She stayed home more, and she loved my friends. Thick-n-Juicy didn't have to stay at Nana's house all the time now. The only thing missing from my life was Ahmad. I hated that I missed him as much today as I did a year ago. . . .

"Still thinking about him?" my mother walked over to me and whispered.

"Yeah." I nodded.

She kissed me on the forehead. "One day the hurt will go away."

"I hope so."

"Dee!" my dad yelled. "I need your help."

My mother's face lit up like Christmas, New Year's, and the Fourth of July all in one. "Your daddy's calling!" she said. "Let me see what he wants. You girls have a good time tonight!" She turned toward the door and then she quickly turned back around toward us.

"I know, Ma," I said before she could say anything. "We'll be home by curfew."

"See?" Her smile sparkled. "I wasn't going to say that. Although you have to abide by your curfew. But what I was going to say is that you all look fabulous!" She winked her eye and her smile lingered behind her.

"I'm so glad she's not sis-in-law-zilla anymore," Keeya said.

"I heard that!" my mother yelled.

"I love you, Deedra!"

"Umm-hmm, I love you too, Keeya."

"Whew, that was close," Ree-Ree said.

"For real." Martini grabbed her purse. "We just got up in here good, Keeya. Dang."

"Whatever." Keeya chuckled. "But anyway, it's time to get our party on!"

"And you know this," Ree-Ree said. "Fa'sho! Hey, remember when we had to rent fake IDs?"

"Stop the press," Martini said, "that was last year and we can drop the subject of renting IDs. I did the best I could do."

The radio filled the car as we drove to Mc-Daniel's Bowling Alley, but we were going inside tonight. The music was pumped as we sauntered into the club. We looked way too cute for words. I wore a fitted pair of jeans, stilettos, and our signature Thick-n-Juicy off-the-shoulder white top with gold lettering. And because this was "Rep Your Crew Night," my girls and I pretty much wore the same gear, with the exception of Martini, who insisted on rocking animal print. But whatever, we were still the flyest clique up in here.

"I need everybody to stand up 'cause it's Gucci Time!" poured from the DJ booth as he dropped Gucci Mane's "Gucci Time." Everybody filled the dance floor and those who couldn't fit danced in their spots. This party was on and poppin' and every time Gucci Mane screamed, "Gucci Time!" we replaced the lyrics with, "It's Thick-n-Juicy Time."

We danced so much and worked the floor so hard that I didn't even see the brick wall I crashed into. "I'm so sorry," I said, as I looked up, and after a few minutes of staring and my mind quickly

putting the pieces together, I said, "Ahmad?"

I was stunned. Seriously. Like I didn't know if I should be happy or indifferent, or act like I didn't know him. Or if I should simply be real and fold into the feeling that filled my heart and caused it to jump around in my chest at the sight of his beautiful face. I could tell by his hesitation that he didn't quite know how to react to me either, but instead of walking away or acting as if he didn't know who I was, he stood there, at least long enough for me to say, "How are you?"

"I'm okay," he said. I expected him to cuss me out or go off, but surprisingly he didn't.

An awkward silence slipped in between us. And, like, I wanted to say more, I did, I just didn't know what to say. "Well, take care," he said, and I felt like he'd beaten me to saying the same thing. And then just like that he was gone. Just that fast.

"Come on, girl," Keeya said, oblivious to what had just happened to me as she danced. "Let's get it!"

The DJ dropped Rick Ross's throwback "B.M.F." and the crowd erupted into a chant of "Big Meech. . . ."

I tried to dance and I wanted to feel as crunked as the crowd and my crew, but I couldn't. No matter what I did or how bad I wanted to act as if Ahmad being here didn't affect me, it did matter. It mattered a lot.

My eyes scanned through the crowd as much as they could, but Ahmad was nowhere in sight. I slid from the center of the dance floor and I spotted him giving his friends dap and heading toward the door to leave.

I watched him as he left out the door and I didn't follow him, because I thought for a second that maybe this was best and that well enough was best left alone. But as quickly as that thought came to me it left . . . and so did I.

"Ahmad," I called him, as he walked out of the bowling alley and into the parking lot.

He turned around and I knew he couldn't exactly tell where my voice was coming from because there was a crowd of people in front of me and the clouds were opening up and delivering rain. I moved to the side of everyone and hoped he could see me through the wet drops. I called him again, "Ahmad. Over here." I waved my hand in the air.

He stopped in his tracks and for a moment I thought he was going to turn back and leave me hanging. But he didn't. I walked toward him and he met me halfway, stopping in front of the Impala. Again there was that awkward silence, and then I said, "I know you probably hate me, and I mean . . . I wouldn't blame you. I know I would probably hate me—"

"Good thing you're not me," he said.

I bit the corner of my lip. "I just want you to know that I loved you and I still do."

Ahmad stared at me as the rain poured from the sky. It drenched us, yet we didn't move, and for the first time ever, it felt as if time were doing us a favor and standing still long enough for us to absorb and share the same moment. No lies between us . . . just the truth, naked and bare.

Ahmad moved closer to me and grabbed both of my hands. "I never hated you, Chance. I didn't. I wanted to, but no matter how much I tried, I couldn't. I loved you too much—"

"So then maybe—"

"Shhh, let me finish. You have a lot of growing up to do. A lot, and I may not hate you, but last year when I stood there with my hands cuffed behind my back and my life flashing before my eyes, I didn't know whether I was coming or going. I was lost and helpless, all because you were too selfish to tell me the truth."

"I'm sorry. I wish I could take back what I did."

"I wish you could too, but you can't."

I hated that tears were filling my eyes. "So is this really good-bye?"

"Good-bye?" He shrugged his shoulders. "Maybe. Maybe not."

"What does that mean?"

"It means that you never know what the future holds." He placed a soft kiss on my lips. "So maybe"—he let my hands go—"I'll see you next lifetime."

THE BOY TRAP

KELLI LONDON

1

August

*M*m. *Mm. Mm. Lovin' him.* Gabrielle shook her head, silently admiring Jay-Sean as he cradled a basketball under his arm, bounced down the stairs, and licked his lips. He gave a head nod to most of his admirers, a pound to some others. For her though, his "Easy Breezy" as he'd affectionately nicknamed her, he spread his delicious mouth into a full smile as he swaggered her way.

"Dang, Breezy. I'd give *any*thing to be in your shoes," Lady, her friend and co-captain of the cheerleading squad, complimented, wearing a shade of red as usual, and bumping into her with thick hips. She popped a Benadryl tablet into her mouth and chewed it. Lady was allergic to anything comprised of energy or atoms or molecules, i.e. everything, and she was also asthmatic.

"Hmph," Tela, Breezy's bestie since their sandbox days groaned, blinking her long, heavy eye-lashes that framed her extra large, artificially col-ored contact-lens-hazel eyes, then hissed, "I know you would if you could, Lady. You're always giving up something."

Lady rolled her eyes. "But not my co-captain spot, Fats!" she sang, calling Tela by the nickname she was trying to shed, and rubbing her second-cheerleader-in-charge status in her face.

"Seems you're not giving up one of your mil-lion allergies either . . . or cookie-dough ice cream," Tela teased.

Breezy tilted her head, gave Tela a please-don't-start look, then turned back to the fine specimen walking their way. "He's a cutie-patootie, isn't he?"

"You ain't *nevva* lied. You got Jay-Sean so open, the only thing he remembers how to shut is those lames on the court. And your man be shut-ting 'em down," another cheerleader added.

"Yessir," Lady co-signed, swinging her wide hips forward as she walked with hands on them. "That's why y'all going to the NBA. Him *and* you." She cupped her palms around her mouth, then called out like a cheer, " 'Cause we . . . what?"

Tela shook her head, crossed her arms, and mumbled, "Loose lips, looser panties. All you want to do is ride Breezy's bra strap to get where you gotta go." Tela's disdain for Lady's fastness showed, just like their love/hate friendship that bordered on jealousy of who was closer to Breezy.

Lady and the other cheerleader broke out in song, doing the old Bankhead Bounce dance. "Hold 'em down now, so they hold us up later!"

That was Breezy's belief and motto on making a guy put a girl up on a pedestal. Do everything you can for your guy to help him get to the top, then reap the rewards when he does. That was the plan: do what her mom did and ride her high school relationship straight to the top, the NBA. She'd have lifetime floor seats, diva-baller status, a McMansion, hundred-thousand-dollar cars with hundred-grand stacks of diamonds to match, and, of course, the pretty babies it would take to solidify her position. She was destined to become a millionaire; her haters could be thousandaires.

Breezy nodded and smiled. "Exactly," she barely answered, looking at her baller candidate, stuck for words. Jay-Sean stood only feet away, and was waving her over to him. A tall, caramel-dipped dream, he had the whitest teeth she'd ever seen, and Doublemint gum breath that always made her pause. He was, without a doubt, the cutest guy on the basketball team and a definite NBA draft pick. "Yes . . . that's my baby right there. I'll check y'all in a few. I'm going in. . . . Gotta talk to my man and see what's up."

"That's wassup," somebody said.

"Work on the new cheer while I'm gone," Breezy instructed.

"I'll work on the cheer while they're drooling,

wishing they were you," Tela said, looking at Lady. Her disgust was obvious. "You might wanna watch her, B. When people want to be you, they want to test out what being you is like . . . like trying on your man or something else you wouldn't normally loan them."

"Get your man, girl," Lady sang, throwing Tela a nasty look, ignoring her. She hoisted up her already-too-short skirt, then pivoted her back toward Tela as if telling her she wasn't worth her time.

Breezy turned around, flinging her long braids over her shoulders. "Oh . . . trust me, boo," she said to Lady, emphasizing each syllable with her French-manicured acrylic nail. "You know I *got* 'im!" She turned her attention back on Jay-Sean, spreading her glossy lips in a smile and switching her hips as she twisted her way over to him.

He licked his lips again, then bit down on the bottom one. His dimples caved into his cheeks. Breezy couldn't help herself. She reached up and inserted the tip of her finger in the left one. Jay-Sean moved his head, reached down and patted her butt like they were teammates. "Let's walk."

Breezy giggled, scanning the school grounds to make sure they had an audience, then threw a glance back over her shoulder to see if her girls were watching. She nodded, then turned to Jay-Sean. "What's up, Mr. NBA?" She laced her arm through his, and leaned into him. Her head barely reached his elbow.

"Nah. Not out here."

Breezy's eyebrows went north. " 'Not out here' *what*? Oh . . ." She loosened her arm from his, snaked her neck, then stepped in front of him. She poked out her butt and let it lead the way as she spun around. "You want this?" He liked the way it lifted her cheerleading skirt, that's what he had told her, and that's what she'd relied on, over and over. Even in hot-pink sweats, like today.

Jay sucked his teeth like he was irritated. "Come on, Easy. Not out here . . . and that's not what I'm talking about." He looked at his shoes, then mumbled, "That's all you think about."

She rolled her neck again, unsure if she'd heard correctly. "*What?* Did you just say that's all I think about? Well, you wasn't complaining last week, or the week before. Last time I checked, we were on the same page."

He sucked his teeth again, exhaling and rubbing his palm over his waves. He looked at her sideways like she'd stolen from him. He grabbed her elbow and guided her to the side of the school grounds.

"Why are you taking me over here—"

"Eeezzzzay! Easy does it?" Doo-Wop, one of Jay-Sean's teammates who Breezy detested beyond belief, called out like an ROTC drill, cutting her off.

"Do it, Eeezzzzay!" some other teammates answered with her nickname.

Breezy reared back her head, curiously looked

at Jay. As much as she couldn't stand Doo-Wop, she broke into a smile and wondered if he was trying to make amends. Either that or everyone seemed to know how much Jay-Sean cared about her. "Why are they singing my name? You told them to?"

He shook his head, began to pace. His frustration became clearer with each step. His problem struck Breezy like a heavy brick.

"Oh, Jay-Sean," she said, walking up closer and rubbing his arm, blocking him from moving. "You didn't hear back from the college scout?" she asked, thinking the university who'd been wooing him since last season had changed their mind about wanting him, but she found that hard to believe. Jay-Sean was beyond a good high school baller, maybe even too advanced for most colleges. If anyone didn't want him, they were out of their mind. Still, the look of disappointment on his face hurt her soul, and she had to find a way to lift his spirits. He was her boyfriend, so any problem of his was also hers. "Well, you know we don't have any problems, just solutions. That's what my daddy . . ."

"It's over, Breezy."

". . . always says." She paused, closed her eyes, swallowed harder than she ever had in her life, and was sure something was lodged in her throat. Had to be with all the trouble she was having getting whatever it was down and out of the way of the words she had to say. "Wha . . . what? What did you just say, Jay-Sean?" she asked, her eyes still closed. She was afraid if she opened them, they'd do something stupid and embarrassing without her permission, like cry.

"I said, 'It's over.' I'm going to another school."

Relief coursed through her. *Whew!* So he hadn't just tried to break up with her. He was talking about basketball. Still, a major problem, but not one she couldn't fix. They were going all the way to the pros, and she was going to make sure of that, just as she'd made sure he was popular and *in*. Before her, he'd only been a basketball player. Because of her, he became a baller, *the* basketball player from Lakeview High. She shook her head. He was putting a noose on her plans. It'd be hard to keep her claws in him if he switched schools, not to mention he'd be jeopardizing her plans for the second-only-to-prom best dance of the year in December. She opened her eyes and breathed deeply. She rubbed her palm on his arm while she spoke. "Okay. I understand, boo-boo. I do. But it's the beginning of the year—you have all the time in the world to tighten up your game. So you don't have to switch schools, you don't. Strengthen your offense, baby. Make the other team play *your* game. You're the point guard; it is *your* game. My daddy says that's all you need to do. That's what got him into the NBA—"

Jay-Sean put his free hand on her shoulder,

shushing her while still cradling the basketball. "No, Easy, that's not it. I'm not quitting." His eyes turned into comical slits and he laughed. "Why would I do that? Never mind the college scouts, Easy. That's a diz-zuhn deal. Done. Finnito. NBA recruiters are already after me." He slapped his hand against his chest. "I just transferred to a school where I can shine more—and name my price. I don't have to finish college to go pro. . . . I don't even have to pay for college. They'll pay me to go. Ain't that sumptin?"

Breezy's eyes beamed. So he'd already transferred, and they *were* going pro. To the NBA just like Lady had said. "Okay. So where?" she asked, wanting to add "are we going?" but didn't. She was the hot topic at school, the high girl up on the totem pole. She didn't beg; people begged her for her reach. She couldn't let him know that she'd bend so easy for him. She had allegiance to her school, but more to her boyfriend and future because she had none without him. So, yes, she'd transfer with Jay-Sean, but it wouldn't be easy, and she didn't want to leave before the December dance. He'd have to coax her, and she'd still have to convince her biggest sponsor, her dad, but she'd do it . . . for him and their NBA career and the plush life with two-point-five kids, she'd agree.

Jay-Sean stepped back from her, dropped one hand to his side, and cradled the ball tighter under his arm. He shrugged. Bit his bottom lip again. "So . . . you feel me, right?"

Breezy smiled and nodded, wondering would the other school's prom be as fire as theirs. Either way, they'd be hot. She'd see to that too.

"I knew you'd understand, Easy Breezy. It's just like I was telling Doo-Wop and 'em, we've always had an understanding. You're just . . ." He shrugged. ". . . easy."

Doo-Wop? Did this knucklehead just say he was talking about me to Doo-Wop?

He wrapped his long arm around her and pulled her to him in a hug. Immediately, she relaxed and rested the side of her face against his stomach. She closed her eyes and breathed in his pre-basketball scent. He smelled so fresh, like soap and baby powder. "I knew you wouldn't make saying good-bye hard. So . . ." he said, releasing her. He held up his fist, tapped it on hers, giving her a pound like she was just some dude off the street, not the girl he'd spent the better part of a year with. "It was good while it lasted, shawty. I'll check you . . . if I can. Cool?"

Check me? If he can? Breezy's heart crashed to her knees, and something either knocked the wind out of her or her ego was rapidly deflating. He loved her. That's what he'd said. *Right?* She panted like a thirsty dog and balled up her fist. He loved her. That's what he'd whispered in her ear while they pretended to be grown and they'd planned what they were going to wear to the prom and how everyone would be jealous of them at the December dance. *He lied*. "What. Did. You. Just. Say. Jay-Sean?"

"Eeezzzzay! Easy does it?" Doo-Wop hollered again, taunting her louder this time.

"Do it, Eeezzzzay!" the Echo Boys sounded off in chorus.

Breezy glanced left, then right. The team was quickly approaching. Her neck cracked as she whipped her head around quickly to look over her shoulder to the sight of tomato red and flashing color-crayon-hazel eyes, two dead giveaways for Tela and Lady. She gulped. Her girls were indeed staring from across the grounds and seemed to be listening too. She knew they were definitely too far away to hear, but she felt like they could hear every word and breath she took. Her heart drummed in her ears, banging tears closer to the surface with each vibration. Jay-Sean's words had cut her too deep, and now she felt exposed. Like a fraud. A classy one though, she reminded herself, trying to catch herself before she slipped in front of him. *Be cool. Be cool. You're important . . . if not to him, to you. Gotta be important to myself*, she soothed herself, talking herself down from straight losing it on him. Unclenching her fists, she exhaled and swallowed her tears.

With all the strength she could muster, she made her arms lift and extend. He may have hurt her, but she wouldn't let him know it. Wrapping her arms around Jay-Sean, she hugged him tight, rocked him side to side, then gave him a pound and a super forced smile. "Wasn't nothing but a thing, chicken wing," the stupidest thing that she could've said tumbled out of her mouth, but she'd heard her father say it so many times, it just came natural. She forced her smile to stretch wider and turned toward her awaiting squad. *Please don't cry*, she silently begged herself as she marched across the grass, swinging her butt like a pendulum. She had to save face. After all, she was Gabrielle Newton, aka Breezy—the hottest girl to ever grace the halls of Lakeview High. *I'm an asset*. She shot one last look over her shoulder to see if he was looking. She hiked her butt farther in the air. *Kiss my asset*, she telepathically told him, and wished he could hear her.

"So what did Wide Open have to say this time? You need me to cover up for you two again . . . one night or two?" Lady sang, laughing. The midsection of her red shirt rose and fell with each chuckle.

Breezy shrugged and threw on her cool. "Nah. That won't be necessary. His moms is making him switch schools, something about a divorce or whatnot. He's going to work to help out, and not sure about college, so I had to let him go. He's fine. A cutie-patootie but . . . you know . . . no college, no NBA," she lied, her voice almost cracking. She caught herself, perked up. "And no NBA, ladies, and no *what*?" she cupped her hands around her mouth and yelled out almost as loud as Doo-Wop and the Echo Boys had sung her name.

"Breezzzzay!" Lady and the other cheerleader sang.

Tela just nodded, looking like she had trouble lifting her false eyelashes and blinking her lids over the contacts.

Breezy shivered. Tela's big, pretty, pop eyes made her uncomfortable because she could feel her sandbox buddy looking straight through her tough-girl charade.

2

September

The bedroom door opened. Feet slapped heavily against wooden floorboards, flip-flopping their way down the hall toward the kitchen. Old-school hip-hop music soon filled her ears, and the smell of bacon wafted into her space, climbed her nostrils, and dove into her empty stomach, wreaking havoc. Breezy wrapped her arms around her middle, wishing she'd eaten dinner last night. But she didn't have time. And now, thanks to her mom's cooking, the front of her belly was kissing the back of her belly, and was hurting between smooches. Glancing up at the wall, she exhaled hard, making her lips sputter as she looked at why she couldn't fit in eating. A blinding trail of fluorescent pink Post-it notes stuck to her wall, reminding her in her mother's handwriting of what she had to do to stay on the cheerleading squad.

Keep up your grades! Rise above a C! A pretty package is only wrapping, the real gift is what's inside! Average is just as close to failure as it is to achievement, so aim higher! You're an asset!!!

Her stomach growled and her eyes shot to the lone fluorescent-green Post-it at the end of the trail of pinks. The only reminder that really made her skip supper so she could spend her evening studying math, her most terrifying subject; writing a marketing plan for a business project; and trying to perfect a new cheer before she'd finally crashed on top of her bed.

Study, Princess. Raise your grades. Stay on the squad or NO money! Love, Daddy.

The flip-flops sounded off again, then the music blared even louder. "Okay. Okay!" she yelled at her mother's idea of gently waking her. "I'm up. . . . I didn't have first period today. Remember?"

She rolled out of bed, snatched up her cell before her feet touched the floor and checked her call log, text messages, and e-mail. "Nada. Nil. And nothing . . . great," she hissed.

It had been more than a month since The Break-up, and she'd only heard from Jay-Sean once. And that was only after she'd "accidentally" called him three times. She'd smartened up after that, putting him on countdown. Her eyes darted to the calendar on the wall, and the big red circle she'd scribbled around today's date reminded her it was official. She was done. Over him. Had pushed that tragedy off the back of the bus to make room for a new passenger. Scrolling through her contacts, she located his name, selected OPTIONS, then erased him. Immediately, he was gone from her phone and life because she knew not one number by heart. Who did anymore?

"And just like that"—she snapped her fingers—"you're a memory." She cleared her throat. "He must've forgotten who my daddy is!" She slammed the phone back on the nightstand. It vibrated before she turned around.

"Easy Breezy, beautiful . . ." she answered, voice still half asleep and deeper than usual.

Tela laughed. "Breezy? I know you didn't just get up. You sound like that old Barry White dude Poppadoppalous be playing during his card games," she said in one breath, referring to her grandfather, her voice blaring like she was as hard of hearing as he. "Nevva mind. Listen, get here immediately! Posthaste! There's something in the gym you need to see." Incredibly, her volume managed to get louder.

Breezy pulled the phone away from her ear and looked at it like Tela's face would appear on the screen in video. Then cautiously, she put it back to the side of her face, careful not to let it touch her skin. She wanted to know what was going on, not go deaf in the process. "What?" she asked, trying to figure out what all the noise was about. "Why are you all excited? And what *is* it?"

"Just get here. Immediately! And you're welcome."

It was way too early for this. Breezy wiped sleep from her eyes, not understanding Tela. What had Tela done for her in the last twenty-four hours that she needed to thank her for? "Remind me why I'm thanking you again, Fats."

"Hurry up and get here, and then you'll see. And trust me; you will thank me, Gabrielle Newton." Tela hung up, making Breezy freeze. No one ever called her by her full name unless it was serious . . . or worse, she was in trouble.

Breezy's sneakers squeaked across the gymnasium floor, quickly coming to a halting stop. A ball of anxiousness, she wanted to roll across the room and touch what her eyes held to make sure she wasn't seeing things. She shuddered, first hot, and then cold. She wasn't in trouble as she had suspected; she was in serious trouble. Mega serious. Her stomach growled from hunger and nervousness, and the longer she watched, the worse it got.

"I told you," Tela said, fluttering her inch-long eyelashes.

Breezy licked her lips. Baby looked like an overpriced movie treat, tempting her more each time he blew by. Sweat glistened on his skin like someone had dipped him in melted butter, and suddenly she craved popcorn. Caramel corn. "He's fast," she said, crossing her arms, watching his skills.

Lady walked up next to her, shaking her head and popping her gum. She took a swig of allergy medicine, threw a red towel over her shoulders, crossed her arms, and bent forward like she wanted to join the game. "More than fast—a candidate. Keep watching."

Something disgusting pulled her attention. "I would if I could, but Doo-Wop's lips keep getting in the way."

Lady cupped her hands around her mouth, and yelled, "Ay! Doo-Wop! Pick up your lips and exit the court."

Doo-Wop flipped the bird.

Baby dribbled the ball and owned the court. He ran. Shook. Called plays and picks. Performed the prettiest layups. Alley-ooped, on accident and on purpose. He was a one-man team. And right then and there, Breezy decided she was going to be his personal cheerleading squad.

"So?"

"Well," Tela sang like an old Southern pastor.

He was a lowercase god, Breezy thought. Had to be. A little Hercules mixed with Adonis, a bit of the original sun god, Helios, and whoever was the athletc god if there was one. "Oh, yeah. Nike," she said to herself, then to her girls, "He's like . . . mmm. He flows like Poseidon."

"Hunh?" Lady asked, her jaw almost hitting her chest.

"Lady, either the bottom of your face is too heavy or there are rocks in your mouth pushing down your chin. Pick up your face. Over there looking like Doo-Wop," Tela urged with a hard-to-read smirk, hitting Lady with an ultimate low blow. Doo-Wop was a joke of a boy with an awful mug and worse attitude. Tela turned her attention back to Breezy and nodded. "Yes, B. H2-oh at its finest. And we're not talking Aquafina either. Told you you'd thank me."

Lady blew out her frustration, then Ping-Ponged her eyes between Breezy and Tela. "See . . . this is the madness I be talking about. That weird mess. Who talks like that but you and *Fats*?" She held up her index finger, wagged it with her words. "What in the *hello* are you talking about? Puh-who and H2O. Water? Let me guess, chemistry?"

Breezy laughed. "We had a Greek mythology class together last year. And that"—she pointed at the stranger on the court—"is a god in the flesh that I did *not* get to study. I want my money back."

Tela rolled her eyes. "Girl, this is public school. You can't get a refund on zero."

"Figures." Breezy shrugged, unable to pull her eyes away from him. Whoever *him* was. "Poseidon. Water god."

Lady put up her hand, and waited for Breezy to high-five it. "Whatever. You can call him what you want, but I say he's just F.I.N.E. In *all* caps. There's no other way to describe him."

Breezy walked away from the court. "All right," she called over her shoulder. "Give me the B.I."

Lady shrugged, removing the red towel from her shoulders, getting ready to wipe sweat from her brow, then paused. "Believe it or not, I don't have one clue about who he is or his business."

Breezy and Tela both did double takes. "What?" they asked in unison, surprised because normally Lady knew everything, including what happened to that ark Noah was coasting before the world ended the first time around.

"I can't always know everything . . . besides I'm fine and these hips were made for—"

"He's point guarding for *our* team," Tela cut her off, her lips spreading like hot peanut butter, looking happy as she upped Lady with sacred information.

Point guarding? Breezy looked at them both like they'd shrunk right before her. "Are you serious? That's it? That's all we know? Fats? You pulled me out of the house for . . . ?" She shrugged.

Lady laughed. "Yep . . . this. You're Breezy. Breeze on over there and make it happen, cheerleading cap'n. Show 'im how we do." She fanned the towel in front of Breezy.

Tela put her hand on her hip and rotated her neck. "He's here. At our school. Playing for our team. What more do you need? All you have is

THE BOY TRAP

time and space." She twisted open the cap on her water bottle.

Breezy tilted her head, swept her braids off her face, and bit her bottom lip. Licking the gloss from her front teeth, she made her eyebrows dance. "Wrong. You forgot one thing, Fats," she said, rifling through her purse.

"Tela. I'm in the twelfth grade. Call me Tela. I'm too old for Fats—and mature. I keep telling you two."

"Whatever." Breezy ignored her. She pulled out a small notebook and pen. She clicked it open. "It's not about time and space. It's about opportunity. Clear a path, ladies," she said, snapping her finger, snatching Lady's red towel and Tela's water, and then sashaying toward the guys. "Opportunity's calling and Breezy's coming through."

With water and towel in one hand, pen and pad tucked under her elbow, she swished her hips across the court. "Time out. Time out! An urgent nonemergency," she announced, yelling and stopping in the middle. "You and you." She gestured toward Doo-Wop, the biggest pain in her butt who was also the school's best forward, and Baby, the lowercase god. "Come here."

Doo-Wop stopped in his tracks and glared as his lips hung. He cringed like someone had stabbed him in the foot, then pointed at himself. "Who ya talking to, Breezy? Me?"

Breezy nodded, sure she could smell his dank breath across the room.

His chin, controlled by gravity, did the unthinkable; it fell even closer to his chest. Unlike Lady's jaw drop minutes before, Doo-Wop's malfunction was permanent. He was a mouth breather. "Aww! Whut!" he shouted, stomping his foot in a male hissy fit. "Don't be calling me, gurl. You know I don't like you, gurl."

Breezy tilted her head and waited for Doo-Wop's production to be over. She knew he'd spazz out and flip; that's why she'd chosen him first. To get him and his trifling attitude out of the way and feed him the information she wanted him to have. Because if she'd learned nothing else while in school, she'd learned that other than his being a pain in her butt, he was a hopelessly nosey gossiper who filled in the blanks as he saw fit. In other words, he was a liar. A big one. "Just come here, Doo-Wop. Dang. I have to get your info for new team jerseys. You do want a new jersey, don't you?" she lied, hoping that Baby, whoever he was, was worth the trouble she was going through. God knew she'd rather walk barefoot through a hot manure field on a humid day than be accosted by Doo-Wop's ever-stinking breath.

Doo-Wop's chin lifted a centimeter as he perked up. " 'Ell yeah. I want a new jersey. Gonna be on the court 'ot to def too," he answered.

"Yeah, you gonna be *hot* all right," she answered, over enunciating, then mumbled, "with your hot, rank breath." She rolled her eyes. Poor Doo-Wop also couldn't pronounce words that started with an H. Breezy assumed it was because it would require him doing the impossible: lifting his jaw all the way.

With the largest hands, feet, and lips she'd ever seen, Doo-Wop made his way to her. "Wassup?"

Breezy reared back her head as far as she could, and almost passed out. She was sure he'd fried her eyelashes with his breath. "Uhm"—she cleared her throat—"I'm gonna need your size, mailing address, and phone number. E-mail too, if you have one. The jerseys are gonna be sent straight from the company . . . courtesy of a sponsor . . . if we can get the sponsor to *sponsor* us. It's kinda like we're entering a jersey lottery," she added, lying, because she knew the players would never receive new jerseys, and she wanted to be covered in case someone pressed her about not having money.

Doo-Wop started rattling off answers, his breath blowing a gust of funk with each syllable.

Breezy threw up her hand. "Stoppit! Stoppit. Stoppit," she urged. "Write it down yourself. Here." She shoved the notebook at him, held her breath, and prayed she wouldn't pass out. Passing out in front of a dude she was trying to pull was so negative sexy. "Hurry," she rushed, still afraid to breathe for fear of inhaling Doo-Wop's exhale.

Doo-Wop took forever to scribble on the paper. He looked up, then around as if searching for something. He wrote something else; then he handed her the pad. She nodded, and tears cascaded down her cheeks. Her watering eyes told her that not only had she been waiting to exhale, she'd also refrained from blinking. *Who has breath like this?*

"You want me too?" the lowercase god jogged up to her and asked.

"Yes . . ." Breezy was grinning so hard, her lips spread almost as wide as Doo-Wop's. Baby's breath was super fresh and he was cute to nth degree. Yes, she thought, I'd like to get up close and personal with you. "Yes. Yes, of course I want you, since you're offering." She removed the red towel from her shoulder and dabbed perspiration from his forehead, then handed him Tela's water. "Have a sip and come talk to me. I need your information for your basketball jersey."

"Okay," he said, following her lead.

She walked over to the bleachers, climbed two rows, and sat. She patted the empty spot next to her.

With one huge step, he was on the same row as she. He sat down and his knee touched hers. He looked at her apologetically, and smiled.

Breezy turned the page in her notepad. She licked her lips and blushed. She hadn't expected to feel so giddy. Here she was, supposedly in control, and with one touch of his knee she'd turned into putty. "What's your name and . . ." she began, but couldn't finish. His just looking at her made her words jumble in her throat. She shrugged, then handed him the pad. None of her exes had ever had this effect on her. This feeling was way new. She cleared her throat. "Can you please write your information down, including phone number and e-mail? Oops, don't forget size. Size is important."

He looked at her with raised eyebrows. He laughed. "That can be taken in a lot of ways, Miss . . . ?"

"Breezy," she answered for him. "The name's Breezy."

He shook his head in the negative. "What's your real name?"

"Gabrielle. But everyone calls me—"

"Breezy. I know, you just told me. Good thing I'm not everyone, I'm Tyler Scott, Gabrielle." He bit his bottom lip, and Breezy almost passed out. His dimples were even deeper than Jay-Sean's, and, as she watched him write down his information on the pad of paper, she saw he had almost perfect penmanship. *Does this dude have any flaws?*

She summed him up in one glance. About six-foot-four. He had a muscular, yet athletic build, and he was clean cut. He rocked a Dark Caesar haircut that had so many waves she got seasick just trying to follow the flow of them. His fingernails were clean and clipped, not bitten and ragged. *Good for touching. Definite plus!* Pretending like she had to retie her shoe, she moved in for the real telltale sign of him being worthy of hanging around. She bent forward and leaned in toward him. He'd been balling something serious, so she didn't expect him to be washing-powder and deodorant fresh, but she needed to see if his sweat was urine funky or I-bathe-daily tangy. Turning her head just slightly, she prepared for the worst and prayed for the best as she inhaled. She stopped. Reared back her head. Popped open her eyes. She was more than surprised. Tyler, even all sweaty, smelled like a dream, like some major-brand athletic powder had already given him an endorsement deal. With that one whiff, her courageous female swagger kicked back in. No longer was she giddy and afraid to speak. She was Breezy.

She reached up and smoothed out his eyebrows. Even those were on point. "So, what time are we getting together later?"

3

October

In less than two weeks she'd had to block six-
point-five girls from pushing up on Tyler. Actually, there were only six who'd actually gone after
him, and another one who was a potential
pusher-upper and, therefore, was the point five
because the cow never pressed him, she'd just
looked like she'd wanted to say something. He
was Breezy's. Period. *"Discussion over"* and
"spread the word," that's what she'd told the ones
jockeying for her position. There was only one
problem: Tyler didn't know he belonged to her
yet. He'd given her all his personal info, including
two contact numbers, zodiac sign, and the last girl
he'd taken seriously. He'd even told her that he
only liked smart college-bound and career-
oriented girls, but he wouldn't give her his time.
He'd blown off her offer to go out on more than

one occasion. Acted as if he wasn't interested, and went out of his way to avoid her advances. Breezy grimaced. Didn't he realize who she was and that the star of the basketball team was supposed to date the head cheerleader?

She slammed her locker shut and looked around. It was just her and her thoughts hanging out in the hallway. Flipping over her wrist, she looked at the time. She had a free period and nothing major to do, and she felt sleep creeping up on her. Sure, she could study, but that'd be too much like right. Plus, she had the craving for an iced-mocha something. She reached into her back pocket and whipped out her cell phone. She sent a text to Tela and Lady, asking them to meet her outside near the exit; then she bounced. She knew she had no business leaving school grounds or tricking off six dollars at the coffee house, but anything was better than doing what she didn't want to. And school, at this hour, fell into the didn't-wanna-do category.

The wind lifted her braids as soon as her feet connected with the gum-spotted sidewalk. The heavy navy door banged shut, and almost caused her to wince. But Breezy played it cool. She knew the trick to not getting caught ditching was to act like you weren't. And, technically, she wasn't skipping class because she didn't have one. *Who schedules people for a free period, anyway?* The phone vibrated in her hand, alarming her. Reminding herself she'd put on her cool and was supposed to be outside, she answered, "Easy Breezy, beautiful . . ."

It was Tela. "I'm almost there. You at the north exit or south?"

Breezy had to stop herself from laughing. Tela was a speed walker and worrier. So she could imagine the perspiration building on Tela's forehead from rushing and anxiety. She'd bet a dollar to a dime that her sandbox buddy's heart was doing the jackhammer. "North. And slow down before you have a heart attack."

Tela blew like a whale. "Whew. How'd you know?" She laughed. "Lady already out there with you? She wasn't in class. . . ."

Breezy shrugged like Tela could see her. "Nah. I haven't seen her all day. . . ." she began, then something caught her attention. *Tyler? Getting into a car?* She craned her neck, made herself taller by inching up on her tiptoes. *With a girl?* "Oh, *hell*o! Nope, not that," she said to herself, then to Tela, "I'll be here waiting, Fats." She hung up. Walking toward the curb, she kept her eyes on the car, hoping to get a better look. She was wishing like crazy that her sight was tricking her and Tyler wasn't with some other girl.

The car drove by and any hopes Breezy had had were crushed. It was Tyler in the car, sitting right beside a girl who rocked oversized Jackie O. sunglasses and had so much hair that Breezy couldn't see her face.

"Oh, dizzam. I was going to ask you what you

were fussing about, but now I see. Was that *your* man and a chick? Some side jump-off?" Tela's voice blared from behind.

Breezy just shrugged and walked as fast as she could. *This is way too embarrassing.*

Tela caught up with her in seconds; then they walked in silence for a couple of blocks. "Look I didn't mean to rub it in. I was just asking."

Breezy shook her head, then turned a corner and crossed the street. "It's no biggie. I'm cool. I saw it too. And we're not official. Yet. We just talk all the time—on the phone," she lied, speeding down the street.

Tela shouldered her messenger bag, breathing hard. "Slow down. You do know how fast you're walking. I'm almost running to keep up. And I'm supposed to be the fast one out of the group—speed wise. Still a virgin," she made her point clear.

"I'm just a little upset. My man—future, is with some girl."

Tela was almost in a full jog by now. They'd made haste down at least four more blocks. "Whateva, B. I know what's up, or should I say, I know what's not up. You don't have to lie to me. I'm your friend, remember?"

"Yeah, I know, Fats—I mean, Tela," she said, turning the corner onto a main street, and colliding face-first into someone. "I'm sorry," she began to apologize, peeling her face from whoever's shirt.

"Easy?"

"Ras. Dizzam, B!" Tela blurted.

Breezy didn't have to look up to know his voice. It was the one she'd heard for almost a year, and had been waiting for what seemed just as long to hear again. The same one that'd whispered sweet lies in her ears after she'd snuck out of her house to get it in whenever he'd asked. "Jay-Sean?" she managed to utter, then looked up and froze.

Jay-Sean met her with deep dimples, full lips she remembered always being butter soft, and a pretty mini Barbie clinging to him like Saran Wrap. "How've you been?" he had the nerve to ask.

"She's been wonderful—without you," Tela stepped in front of Breezy and said.

Breezy moved Tela back. "I'm good. Who's *she*?" She gave the girl a once-over and decided she wasn't so pretty.

"*She* is his girlfriend," Barbie said, "of almost a year . . . and his future college sweetheart, too. Isn't that right, honey?" the girl said to Jay-Sean.

"College" hit Breezy in the chest like a hammer, almost knocking the wind out of her. Two years ago, her first boyfriend, Dez, traded her in for college, and now Jay-Sean. But his news came with a bonus: Barbie. She could feel her ego deflating again. Puckering her lips, she sucked her teeth and painted on a smile. She tilted her head to the side, cracking her knuckles. "A year. Really?"

Barbie became animated. Happy. Clueless. "Yes. A whole year . . . next week. Right, honey?" she asked a frozen-in-place Jay-Sean. "We just finished picking out our prom stuff. Can you believe it took him months to decide if he was wearing a tux and vest or whatever? We've only been going over the colors and details since February. I know it's soon, but we can never be too early to get our prom colors right," she rattled.

Breezy's eyes were locked on Jay-Sean's while his girlfriend babbled nonstop. "A year? February?" Breezy asked him. They were together last February. Exclusive, she'd believed. Tears welled up in her eyes. But she wasn't hurt. She stopped hurting weeks ago. She was angry. Three-hundred-and-eighty-degrees-hot angry.

Jay-Sean shrugged. A flash of fear shown in his eyes. Fear and begging.

"A year!" Breezy yelled.

Barbie stopped talking.

Tela inched forward, putting herself between Breezy and the loving prom-and-college-bound couple.

Jay-Sean seemed to be stuck for words.

"A year, Jay-Sean?" she barked again. "You were with *her*? A year? Prom? Now college? What next, NBA?" Breezy raked her eyes at Barbie. "Your dream is deferred, *honey*! Unless you're gonna choose to be stupid. You and him weren't to-gether a year because we—me and him—were together. Together-together. Hooking up all the time! Getting it in. Being grown. Feel me?"

Jay-Sean suddenly came to life. "You're trip-ping! Me and you were never a couple. You weren't ever my girl," he said to Breezy, then grabbed Barbie by the arm. "She's tripping. Come on, baby. That's the one that let Dez hit, then he shook her. You know I only like smart girls. She's a groupie."

Barbie protested as she and Jay-Sean disappeared around the corner. Breezy ran after them, but Tela caught her by the back of the shirt, and snatched her back. She wrapped her in a sisterly hug. "Don't play yourself, B. You have too much class to be clowning out here in the streets. And besides, you know the truth about what you and Jay-Sean had."

Breezy exhaled, removed herself from Tela's hug, then walked. She needed air, a break. *A life. A new boyfriend*. A new guy would help her forget Jay-Sean, she thought, returning back to school, the last thing on her mind. She pulled out her phone, and contemplated calling Lady to see what else she could get into, then decided against it. If Lady was free, she'd have returned her text by now.

"Wow," Tela whispered. "You sure you want coffee?"

Breezy looked up, saw that the coffee house was house-party packed. "Nah. It's not that serious. Besides, I'm hungry. Wanna grab a slice and a slushie?" she asked, already knowing Tela's answer and heading farther down the block to the pizza place.

"I think you need to try out for track," Tela teased, catching up.

"Sorry. I can't help it." She stopped in front of the pizza place on the corner, looked at its shoulder-to-shoulder customers, and shrugged. It was around lunchtime, so she knew just about everywhere would be packed. Her stomach growled. "Pizza it is. You play one line, I'll stand in the other. First one to a register orders for both. Cool?"

Tela laughed. "B, I know how this goes. I made up that rule like forever ago." She opened the door and they went in, getting in wherever they fit in.

Breezy carried the slices to a small bistro table in the corner, then set them on the table, and sat down. Tela put their drinks down. "Salt?" Breezy asked.

Tela sat in the seat across from Breezy's, going through the condiments on the table. "Check."

"Garlic powder?"

"Check, check."

"Red pepper flakes?"

"Check, check, check."

"Parmesan cheese?"

Tela shook her head.

"Parmesan cheese?" Breezy repeated.

"Am I supposed to say check too, Gabrielle? Or check, check, check, check?" the most delicious voice she'd heard all day asked.

Breezy whipped her head around, looked up and almost got seasick. There were those waves again. The ones she'd been trying to touch since she'd saw him. The same him who wouldn't give her his time. Tyler. He stood there wearing a pizza-sauce-stained apron and a smile, and held a parmesan cheese shaker in his hand. "I saw Tela. . . . I'm sorry, that is your name, right?" he asked Tela, but his eyes never left Breezy.

Tela giggled. "Yes, it is."

Breezy kicked her under the table.

"Well, Gabrielle, I saw Tela moving the shakers around, so I figured you'd need this. I was just re-filling them in the back." He set down the cheese and raised his eyebrows like he had something else to say or was expecting something.

"Thank you, Tyler. I didn't know you worked here. How'd you manage to—"

"I only have to go to school part-time. I'm ahead. Long story. What are you doing later?"

Now she knew she was going to pass out. Was he asking her out? After she'd done everything she could to get his attention, including flat-out asking for it. Maybe, just maybe, she'd heard him wrong. "Can you repeat that? Because I think you just asked about my availability, which would be next to impossible after . . ." She stopped and caught herself. Tela was sitting across from her, and she had to save face, hold on to some sort of dignity.

Tyler nodded. "I know what I asked you. That's the point. *I* asked *you.* Some of us dudes—even athletes—were raised with some sort of respect, to be men. So . . . what's your availability, Gabrielle?"

Tela sat up, stuck her head in their view, and raised her hand like she was in the class she'd just skipped. "One question, Tyler. Who was that girl you were with in the car a few minutes ago? The one, I assume, who brought you here to work."

Tyler laughed. "Girl?! She'd love that. That *girl* is my mother."

"Then, the answer is yes. She's free later. Right, *Gabrielle*?" Tela sang her given name, rubbing in the fact that Tyler was allowed.

Breezy raised her eyebrows, and licked her lips. Tyler was scrumptious. Delicioso. Soon to be hers. "I'm not free, cheap, or easy. Well, I am Easy, but not like that. I'm also available later."

4

_____

November

"I won't tell if you won't tell," Breezy sang to the full-length mirror while she pinned up her braids. Puckering her lips, she raised her arched eyebrows, putting on her sexy-girl look. Blinking slowly, she eyed her outfit. Her dull-mustard strapless shirt looked good against her cappuccino skin, and her bra fit just right, hiking up her twin towers until they almost looked like too-perfect implants. She nodded in approval, turning until she could see herself from behind. Low-rise, fitted jeans that rode her hips and accentuated what she believed was her best asset announced what she didn't feel she needed to verbalize. She was the greatest. Weren't any ifs, ands, or buts about it.

"Why are you sticking out your butt like that?"

her mother asked her from the doorway, shocking Breezy.

Remember to act cool. "I thought I saw some-thing . . . a spot," she recovered, and walked toward her mom. She turned her back to her mother, then stuck out her butt again. "Do you see something?" She held her breath to prevent herself from laughing while her mom checked.

"No. I don't see anything. Maybe it's the lights and reflection. Where do you plan on going with those tight jeans on anyway? That doesn't look like a movie outfit to me. And what's up with the summer shirt in fall?"

Breezy stood straight, and had to catch herself. She almost rolled her eyes, but decided against it because she liked seeing *and* having a head attached to her body. She knew if she disrespected her mom in any way, she'd get her eyes slapped down her throat and her head knocked into next week. Not that her mother had ever made good on her violent physical threats, but Breezy knew her mom could, would, and had done some drastic things in the past to hurt her, like taking away the cell phone, debit card, and freedom.

"We're going skating, Mom. We did the movies last time. And I have this funky seventies patchwork jacket I'm wearing with this, and the pants aren't really that tight. They're new, so they'll loosen up. Plus, Daddy gave me the jacket for my birthday last year, so I thought it'd be nice to finally rock it so he can see it when he picks me, Fats, and Lady up from the skating rink."

Her mother's face tightened when she mentioned her dad. All it took was Breezy saying his name to make her mother uncomfortable. They'd been divorced forever, but you couldn't tell. Not with the way they hated each other. They didn't even talk, which was fine with Breezy because it made her life and lies simpler.

"Oh. Okay. I'll be leaving right after you. You have any money? Oh—never mind. I forgot, with your dad you won't be needing any. Is *she* coming with . . . never mind that too," she said, referring to the other thing that caused her mother's stress level to rise: her dad's much younger girlfriend who'd just graduated from girlfriend to pregnant fiancée. "I shouldn't have asked." She walked up to Breezy and wrapped her in a hug. "Be good, Gabby. I'll be back on Sunday to pick you up."

Breezy cringed. She hated "Gabby." She squeezed her mother tight, then kissed her on the cheek. "I'm always excellent." *At hiding what I do and not being found out.* "I know you're going to work, but enjoy yourself. Oh, yeah, Mom? Didn't Daddy tell you that *he's* dropping me off Sunday night?"

Her mother tried everything she could not to roll her eyes, but failed horribly. Breezy was sure her mom's baby browns were going to roll out of her sockets and onto the floor. She tightened her lips and managed to squeeze out, "*He* didn't tell me anything. He texted me. As if texted is a word."

Breezy went deaf. She had managed to drown out her mother and make her way out the house and was now trying to think about Tyler, but Lady wouldn't let her do it in peace.

"Did you kiss him yet?" That was Lady, forever inquiring about the unmentionables.

Breezy shook her head, and inserted the key into the lock. She opened the door and entered the alarm's secret code, disarming it. "You're the only person who breaks into their own house. Did you know that?" Tela said, following Breezy inside. "I thought your mom changes the code when she's away and you're supposed to be at your dad's."

Lady closed the door behind them.

Breezy took off her shoes, placing them at the side of the door. "She does. She changes it to the same 'secret' code all the time, but there's nothing secret about it. I captured her on video doing it. It was just as simple as having my dad drop us off at Lady's, then catching a cab here."

"And that was brilliant!" Lady complimented. "Especially since no one was at my house to see us come or go. And your timing is perfect."

"I know. But you know I wasn't coming in here until I knew my mom made it to her destination. That's why I called her at the hotel she checked into—she could be anywhere on her cell."

"Brilliant again!"

Tela shook her head and rolled her eyes.

"Whatever, Fats. You're so dang judgmental. So . . . Breezy, did you? Did you kiss him yet?" Lady asked again, crossing her legs into a meditation position on the floor.

Breezy shook her head.

"See, I knew it. Fats, I told you!" Lady said, holding out her hand. "Pay up!"

Breezy was still shaking her head. "I don't kiss and tell. You know that, Lady."

Lady crossed her arms and snaked her neck. "Bull. You do too tell. You told me about you and Dez, and Jay-Sean."

"I did not."

Tela huffed. "Maybe Dez and Jay-Sean told you . . . behind closed doors."

Breezy's head spun, bounced back, then spun again in a double take. "What?"

Lady unfolded herself from the floor. "What's that supposed to mean, Fats?"

"Stop calling me Fats, trick!"

Breezy held out her arms. "Okay. Enough. You two are going to ruin my night before I get it started." She hugged each one of them. "Lady, I'm at your house tonight. Tela, I'm at yours tomorrow. We'll all get up for real tomorrow. Cool? And don't kill each other on the way home. . . . Oh, I forgot, you're besties whenever I'm not around. I don't understand that!"

Breezy walked them to the door, let them out,

then locked herself inside. She was alone in her home for the whole weekend like she was grown.

And if she had her way, she'd be doing grown-up things with Tyler tonight. Immediately, she ran for her cell phone. It was going to be the night, she was sure. She and Tyler had been hanging steady for a few weeks, and they acted like they were together. It was time to make it official.

As soon as he answered the phone, she melted. His voice was smooth and clear, almost as deep as a grown man's. "So what's up for tonight?" she asked, lying down on her bed.

"Gabrielle . . . you sound good. Happy. I was going to call you tonight." He avoided her question.

Breezy lay across her bed, tracing her fingertip along the pattern of her royal purple spread. She smiled. Giggled. Grinned harder. "So you were going to call me, but you won't tell me if you have plans tonight?" she asked, rolling over onto her back and waiting for his answer. She crossed her legs at the knee, and played with her braids.

Silence.

"Stop frontin' like you don't hear me, Tyler."

He laughed. "What're you wearing, Gabrielle?"

Breezy sat up, looked out into the hallway. Scooting to the edge of the bed, she got up and closed her bedroom door. She knew her mom was away and she was alone, but talking like this with the door open didn't feel right. "Why do you ask?" she whispered into the phone. "What do you want me to have on?"

Tyler laughed. "Clothes, Gabrielle. I was going to call you to see if you wanted to hang out tonight. You're a trip, talking all low and sexy."

He was on his way, that's what she kept telling herself. She ran through the house looking for something to straighten up to help soothe her nervousness, but there was nothing to clean. Both she and her mom were neat freaks, borderline obsessive-compulsives. Breezy looked in the mirror for the millionth time. In ten minutes, she'd changed clothes three times, wanting to look perfect for Tyler. But in her mind, nothing was good enough for him. She looked at the clock. Shook her head. Zipped toward the bathroom and turned on the shower. He was due to arrive in fifteen minutes, and she had to be almost ready. *Almost* being the operative word, the one she was banking on to help her fulfill her Hollywood-movie-like vision of them falling madly in love. They'd be doing the forever-after thing with him as the star NBA player and her as the perfect model wife.

"I'm tripping," she said, stepping into the shower and lathering up for the second time tonight. She wasn't dirty, and didn't feel like it. She was bathing for effect. While rinsing off, she thought she heard something. Tilting her head sideways, she turned down the water, listening. The doorbell chimed.

She stuck her head out of the shower, and yelled, "One second!" She grabbed her towel, hopped out, and ran toward the front door, dripping wet. "One second," she said again, haphazardly wrapping the towel around her. With a glance through the peephole, she opened the door, and there he was.

"Hi . . ." he began, then stopped. His mouth was gaping open.

Breezy played it cool. "Sorry, Tyler," she said, walking toward her bedroom. "I'm running late. Come in. Have a seat." She hurried down the hall. "There's stuff to drink in the fridge." She closed the door to her bedroom behind her and leaned against it. Her heart was pounding and her feet were cold.

"I can come back in a few minutes, if you want me to, Gabrielle," his voice sounded through her door.

She shook her head as if he could see her. That's not what she'd been aiming for. She was certain that by now he'd be down the hallway and halfway inside her bedroom. "*No!* You're fine. I'll be out in a sec. I would've been finished and dressed by the time you got here, but the hot water just disappeared. . . . I don't know what happened to it, but I couldn't rinse off until it warmed up." She dried off while she lied, then stepped into the sexiest panty and bra set she owned and lay her body across her bed. "Tyler," she yelled, "can you come here, please? I need your help."

Silence.

"Tyler! Don't start. I'm not naked! Come here, please."

His footsteps announced he was on his way. Slow and heavy, his feet took their time coming to her aid. It wasn't going at all like she'd imagined. Usually tall and athletic guys could make it to her in a few steps, but not Tyler. He was proving himself just the opposite of Dez and Jay-Sean. They'd been eager, and she hadn't had to try so hard, most times not at all.

His knuckles wrapped softly against the door.

"Come in," Breezy sang without lifting her head. "Can you lotion my back, please?" she asked, not turning over or looking at him.

Silence collided with a big pregnant pause.

"Tyler?" she asked, her head still down. It felt like time had stood still and they'd entered another dimension, went through a warp hole or something strange like the movies her dad watched.

"Yes, Gabrielle . . . I'm here. I don't know if it's such a good idea, though."

Now she turned to look at him, propping herself up on her elbows. "What's not a good idea, and why not?" she asked, trying to look as innocent as possible.

Tyler smiled and shook his head. "You're a trip.

THE BOY TRAP

Me, being in here with you—naked—is what's not such a good idea."

Breezy laughed. "Why, Tyler? I make you nervous. You must be attracted to me or something. What?" She bit her lip. "And I'm not naked . . . unless . . . is that your way of telling me that that's what you want, me naked?"

Tyler shook his head in the negative and exhaled. He picked up the lotion and squeezed some into his hands. Breezy turned back over, laying her head on the bed and closing her eyes when she felt him near. Warm tingles moved through her when he began to rub the lotion on her back. In seconds, he was done and almost out of her bedroom. "I'll be out front waiting on you," he said from her doorway.

Breezy's head almost spun off her neck, she'd turned so fast. For a second, she felt the slightest bit of shame move through her. Did she turn him off and disgust him that much? She stood up and gave herself a once-over in the full-length mirror. She had the body of a model. Forget the airbrushed girls on magazine covers; they weren't real and didn't have any meat on their bones. Breezy was fleshed out, not pencil thin and hungry looking. With attitude, she turned and walked the way Tyler just had.

"What's the problem? I'm not good enough for you?" she asked, walking up to the sofa where he sat.

He raked his eyes over her body. "It's not me

you need to be worried about. And, of course, you're good enough—"

Before he could finish his sentence, Breezy had climbed on him and kissed him. She closed her eyes and warmed as he kissed her back. This is what she'd been waiting for. This would seal the deal and answer any unspoken questions she'd had about them being together.

Suddenly he did the unthinkable. He pulled away. "Wait. Wait."

"Wait what?" Breezy asked.

"Look at you. . . ."

Breezy looked down at her panty and bra set. "And? What? You don't like me . . . or you just don't like girls . . . ?"

Tyler pushed her off him. He laughed. "What's my middle name? My favorite color? What do I have to drink before or after a game?"

Breezy caught her balance, almost falling. "What?!"

Tyler stood up. "That's my point, Gabrielle. You don't even know me . . . and, of course, I like girls. Why wouldn't I? Because I'm not trying to hit? What's that, some girl reverse-psychology stuff? Really?" He bore into her while he spoke.

Breezy paid as much attention to her feet as she possibly could. Lifting her head and looking into his eyes was way too embarrassing. She'd never been so flat-out, in-her-face rejected.

He reached out, lifted her chin. "Look at me, Gabrielle."

She did as he asked. "It's like I said earlier, it's not me you need to be worried about being good enough for. It's you. First, you have to be good enough for yourself."

Breezy sucked her teeth. Now he was getting on her nerves. Who was he, anyway? She turned her head, and gave him the side eye.

"You're beautiful and don't know it."

That was it. *Wrong*. She was Easy Breezy and beautiful. She'd turned that phrase at least twice a day, and not only because it sounded good, it was her truth. She shook her head, stabbed his eyes with her glare. "What do you mean I 'don't know it'? I know that just as well as I know my name."

"What's your name?"

"Breezy," she began, then caught herself. "Funny."

Tyler shook his head. "Gabrielle, there's a difference between being pretty and being beautiful. You know you're pretty—you can look in the mirror and see that anytime. Beauty isn't always reflected in mirrors." He bent forward and kissed her on the cheek. "Can I call you later?"

5

Still November

"We're gonna rock right now! We're Warriors and we came to get down. . . ." Breezy threw up her hands and stepped off the pyramid of cheerleaders. Her lower body folded into a V as she fell into the strong waiting arms of their only male squad member. "From school to school we're known, so you better come hard or stay home!"

Lady jumped up and down in place. "Aww! You killed that one, Breezy. Kill't it!" she repeated when her feet met the ground.

Breezy smiled. "I know. I remixed this old-school hip-hop Rob Base joint my mom likes to play in the morning. So, it's my words, Rob's flow. I can't take all the credit."

Tela stepped up, her long eyelashes slowly batted.

Loud, thunderous hand claps sounded off from behind. Breezy turned and locked eyes with Tyler. She sneered at him, almost asked if he was trying to be funny. Since that night at her house, her words for him were limited, and she'd refused to talk to him. She still liked him, but she didn't want to. Besides, she was tired of digging dudes who weren't digging on her the same. If she wanted a headache, she didn't have to date a knucklehead; she could just run into a wall. It'd be less stressful than having the boy blues.

Tyler shrugged and looked at her without expression. He tipped his head to the right, indicating she should look that way. "I didn't clap," he said.

Breezy's eyes followed to where he was gesturing. Mr. Spalding, the boys' head coach and her cheerleading coach's boss, was beckoning her over. *What now?*

"C'mere, Gabby. I need to see you for a second," he said, his lower gums looking like someone had rubbed dirt on them.

She drug her feet, hesitant to talk to him. He was authority, and outside of her parents, she didn't do authority very well. "Hi, Mr. Spalding. What's wrong, now? Someone's shoes too low and eyebrows too short?" she sang, being smart-alecky. The last time he'd intervened with the cheerleaders was when he'd somehow forgotten that they were supposed to wear short skirts; he'd believed their uniforms should've hung to their knees like in his day . . . *when dinosaurs still roamed the earth*.

Mr. Spalding stepped outside of the black foul line, ran his hands through his pretend hair, and then scratched his completely bald head. He bit his bottom lip and looked like he wanted to spit out the snuff he thought no one could see tucked behind his lip. "No, Gabby. I'm afraid it's you, this time," he said, handing her a slip of paper. "This just came down from the office. That spaced-out guidance counselor, who thinks she's a warden, sent you a faint-pink slip—meaning you're not all the way out, just on your way. It seems your grades are too low for you to even think about cheering." He fixed his pretend hairdo again. "How did you manage to fall under a two-point-oh? You can sleep and still score higher than that."

Time stood still for seconds. "What?" Breezy asked. Did he just kick her off the squad? That couldn't be—she *was* the squad. "I can't cheer? Is that what you're saying? My daddy's gonna kill—"

Spalding snatched the sheet of paper from her hand, held it close to his eyes, then moved it away until he seemed to be able to focus enough to read it. "Yep. Pretty much . . . unless you can pick up this math grade."

Breezy did a double take, looking at him. " *'Pick up'* my grade?"

Spalding laughed. "Yep. 'Cause you've certainly

dropped it. You're not just failing math, seems like you don't even know what it is. So you need to pick it up—a book. Figure it out."

Breezy gave him a blank stare.

The invisible hair was in his eyes again. "Got an idea," he said, snapping. "Scott, get over here!" he yelled, calling Tyler by his last name.

Breezy looked from Spalding to Tyler, shrugging to let him know she had no idea what Mr. Spalding was up to.

"Gabrielle, this here is Tyler Scott. He's going pro. For now, he's our star player and, fortunately for you, a genius. He's also nice. He's not even supposed to be here, but he's staying for basketball season . . . so more scouts can recruit him. Anyway, Scott here is gonna tutor you."

"What?" they both sang in unison.

"Yes, son. What else do you have to do? Graduation's not until May, and you only have one class. Besides, this here is our head cheerleader, the finest cheerleading captain ever—she just don't know diddly-squat 'bout math, and her daddy's *very* generous to the school's P.E. department . . . so we *gotta* take care of her." His dirt-brown snuff was peeking out from behind his bottom lip again and his invisible hair was blowing into his eyes. "So . . ." He tossed his head to the side, moving the not-there strands from his face. "I guess y'all gonna be joined at the hip until she raises her grade. And it'll give you more starting time to play for the scouts," he threw in as an incentive for

Tyler. "It's a date. Tonight at six o'clock sharp meet Tyler at his job. He'll tell you where it is."

Breezy paced in front of the pizzeria, checking her text messages and waiting for Tyler to come outside. She was frustrated, double embarrassed, and had to come up with some believable excuse to tell her dad about her declining grades. Her phone buzzed in her hand. She looked at the screen, grabbed a heavy white plastic chair, and sat at the outside bistro table. She looked at the text from Tyler, and decided it was best to get comfortable.

NBA TY: ALMOST DONE. WANNA SLICE?
NO. I'M COOL.
NBA TY: TANTRUMS AREN'T A GOOD LOOK ON U.
NEITHER IS WAITING.
NBA TY: LOOK UP.

Breezy raised her eyes from the phone screen and a smile forced her to spread her lips. Tyler was walking toward her with a big white chef's hat on, holding a pizza over his head with one hand and balancing drinks on a tray with the other. "You know you look like Chef Boyardee, right?"

Tyler laughed. "And you're going to look like this pizza or these sodas if you don't help me out. I'm not a waiter; I can't balance these for too long."

Breezy stood up, then relieved him of the drinks.

He set the pizza on the table, and began pulling condiments out of his pockets. "Check. Check-check. Check-check-check. That should be it—" He snapped his fingers. "Almost forgot your salt." He reached into his front pocket and pulled out a shaker. "Quadruple check. They don't keep this stuff outside because it always comes up missing."

Breezy smiled, pulling sanitizer from her purse. "Who steals salt?"

Tyler turned a chair around backward, then straddled it. He shrugged. "Might be for the containers. Where's your books?"

Now it was time for her to be silent. She'd been so rattled over having to meet him, the last thing she'd thought about was books or math, for that matter. A silly smirk painted her face.

Tyler looked like he was trying to redefine exasperated with his exaggerated breathing and look. He shook his head. "Don't tell me you didn't bring your book, Gabrielle?"

Breezy shrugged a little. "Sorry?" she tried, hoping it'd be enough. "I promise I will next time. I just didn't want to come see you. . . . I wasn't comfortable. You know what I mean. After the last time . . . you know."

Tyler nodded. "I'll give you a pass this time, but after today I can't be responsible. It's your grade." He picked up a slice of pizza, ready to dig in.

"Oh, hold up a sec. We gotta decorate that if

you're gonna eat it." Breezy picked up the cheese and garlic and began shaking them on his slice, then finished with the other two spices. She finished by seasoning her own.

Tyler bit his slice, then closed his eyes in appreciation. He moaned. "This is good."

Breezy smiled. "I know. There are some things I do know how to do right, you know?"

Tyler stopped chewing and looked at Breezy. "Tell you what. Let's eat, then hang out and talk. Let's get to know each other better today . . . maybe learn my favorite color and what I have to drink before and after a game."

Breezy smiled and nodded. She liked where Tyler was going with this. Maybe he was genuinely interested in her after all.

"Okay. What's your middle name?" He winked.

They sat and ate and talked until their mouths were dry and their sodas were empty. Breezy laughed, twirled her braids, blushed, and almost cried from the honesty. She'd opened up to Tyler, and, in turn, he'd opened up to her, explaining he could only drink soda, water, or one-hundred-percent juice because he was allergic to a common sports drink additive. He even ventured into his soft spot—his father's death and his appreciation of his mother and her raising him alone. Breezy didn't believe she'd ever met a more forthcoming person. Tyler was a borderline genius like Coach Spalding had said, and an excellent basketball player headed to the top. Yet, he was humble and seemed not to have an ounce of unnecessary pride.

"So, what's your deal, Gabrielle? You know me. Let me know you."

This is the part she wasn't looking forward to. Her "deal" hurt her feelings and confused her. "Well, my parents met when they were younger than us. My dad went on to college, married my mom, and then was drafted by the NBA. My mom had me somewhere during that timeline. My dad also lost his contract because he got hurt, and they divorced . . . maybe because he lost his contract. I dunno. He also started this huge nonprofit organization to help teens—I'm way proud of him for that. And let us not forget, they hate each other with a passion."

Tyler stood slightly, then leaned over the table. He brushed back her braids from her face, and readied himself to kiss her. "May I?"

Breezy blushed and nodded.

He moved in, brushing his soft lips across her cheek. It was then that she felt the wetness on her skin. Tears had formed and escaped her eyes while talking about her parents. Normally, she would've felt stupid and vulnerable knowing she'd accidentally cried in front of someone—she was Easy Breezy, she wasn't supposed to cry. But it was different with Tyler.

He swept his large hand across her face, drying the tears, and then he sat back in his seat. "I knew you were beautiful. . . ."

She drew her eyebrows together. "Crying makes me beautiful?"

"No. Your honesty does. For the first time since we met, I can tell you're a person." He was silent for a second while he stared at her. "So . . . what are you doing next month? Want to go to the dance with me?"

"You do realize it's a couple's dance? It's no written rule. . . . It's just the way it is."

Tyler nodded and licked his lips. "So . . . would that be a yes or no?"

6

December

There was a problem. Breezy grabbed the over-sized Louis bag she'd borrowed from her mom, and plunged her hand inside until her nails scraped the bottom. She rifled around until she found her house keys, then pulled them out and tossed them aside onto the bed. Immediately, she went back in, located her blot powder compact, and flung it on top of the key ring. Her iPod Touch was next.

She breathed loudly and plopped down onto the bed. She was feeling major defeat and didn't want to cry. Her world was ending. A catastrophe. "Over!"

"Did you find it yet?" Tela asked from the door-way, panting like she'd run a marathon.

All Breezy could do was shake her head. Why was this happening?

"I called Lady. . . ."

Breezy looked sideways at her best friend in the whole world, then threw up her hands like *Why?*

"Well, we were together yesterday, and you can't remember the last time . . ."

". . . I saw it. I know, don't remind me." She stared at the wall, a bundle of nerves. She'd lost her lifeline to the world as she knew it. Her phone was missing. "I'm supposed to be hooking up with Tyler tonight. How am I supposed to do that now? I don't know his number."

Tela walked all the way into the room and released her lithe frame onto the bed next to Breezy. The mattress bounced. "Hooking *up* hooking up? Or just *meeting* hooking up?"

Breezy rolled her eyes. What difference did it make? Either way, neither would happen because she couldn't call him and didn't know where to meet him. Her answer was a shoulder shrug. "Family *barbecue* hooking up. You know Tyler is stingy with his—"

Tela squealed like a stuck pig. She grabbed Breezy's wrists and pulled them both up from the bed. Jumping up in place, she said, "Serious! B, do you know what that means?"

Breezy hopped up and down just for the sake of it. She didn't get Tela's excitement and wasn't about to pretend she did. All she knew was her phone was missing. She planted herself firmly on the ground.

"Stop being such a party pooper. It means you're in, B! You're in. No dude has a girl meet his family unless that girl's *in*. Get it? *In!*"

Breezy thought about it for a second. She and Tyler had been inseparable for weeks. They'd spent countless hours together helping her study math, and she studied him when he wasn't looking. They'd even rocked on the phone until the wee hours of the morning, talking about everything and sometimes nothing, and his nothings were just as interesting. He was a genius, pure and simple, and she'd started to mimic his intelligence to keep his attention, but all she could do was emulate. To master it, she'd have to really study and grasp what she'd pretended to while with him. He had big dreams of going to college, and she'd acted interested in applying. She shrugged. Somehow she'd convinced him that she was university bound, and that's all that mattered. He believed her. So maybe Tela was right. "I guess so, hunh? I'm *in*. We gotta find my phone. Now!"

The girls rifled through the house like burglars, turning things over as they made their way from room to room. Tela put her hands on her hips, scanned the room, and cleared her throat. "B! Look around."

Breezy stopped in her tracks. Instead of looking like they were in the middle of the living room, they looked like they were in the middle of a war zone. Stuff was everywhere. "Oh gawd."

Tela nodded. "I know. This is ridiculous."

"All this mess we made . . . and still, no phone?" she said, putting her hands on her hips. She made a sour expression.

"*Ill*. Not the lemon face. I wasn't referring to the phone—or lack of one," Tela said, her lashes batting slowly.

Breezy picked up a throw pillow from the floor and flung it across the room where it belonged. "Okay, so spill it. I see you over there batting your lashes like they weigh fifty pounds. You always blink slow when a lot's on your mind."

Tela tsked. "You. Look at you. Look around. Are we really going through all of this for a boy? Again? First it was Dez, then Jay-Sean. Now Tyler? Hooking up is not the hook-up, B. . . . You should know that by now."

Breezy looked at Tela like she'd morphed into an alien right before her eyes. If she had, it wouldn't have caught Breezy by as much of a surprise as the stupidity that had just jumped out of Tela's mouth. How could she not understand that Tyler was different? "It's not that serious, Tela."

"That's what I'm trying to get you to understand. What's wrong with waiting?"

"Nothing, if that's what you want to do, *Fats*. But I've waited long enough. . . . Not everyone's a virgin, you know?"

A knock on the door caused them both to stiffen. Breezy's eyes shot to the clock on the mantel. Her mother wasn't due home for hours, and she had a key so there was no need for her to knock.

"Lady?" Tela asked.

"Has to be," Breezy said, then turned her attention to the door. "Lady, just a sec!" she yelled, trying to step over the mess that she and Tela had made.

"It's not Lady, Gabrielle. . . . It's me, and I think this is your phone out here. . . ." Tyler's voice came through the door, trailing off as if he wasn't sure if it was her cellular or not.

Breezy's body froze and her eyes begged Tela's cooperation. So, he'd found her phone, but what was he doing at her place? "Tyler?" she yelled to the door.

"Sorry. Didn't want to pop up, but you didn't answer your phone. . . ."

"It's okay," she answered, then turned to Tela, "Help me, Fats. Please. I can't let him see this house like this. He might think me and my mom are undercover dirty. . . . It didn't look anything like this the last time he was here," she whispered, then turned toward the front door, relieved to know her phone was right outside, but also very anxious. His coming unannounced to her house was definitely a surprise, but how else could he come? There was no way for him to contact her. "Almost ready, Tyler. I have to get *all* the way dressed before I answer the door this time," she lied, knowing he'd appreciate her being so understanding and not so loose like the last time.

"Promise me you won't sleep with him, Breezy, and I'll help you clean up," Tela whispered.

A genuine smile spread on Breezy's face and her fingers crossed behind her back. "Promise."

She was twisted. Literally. Breezy sat on the porch with her legs crossed yoga style, her micros woven into two long Pocahontas braids, and her heart spiraling out of control as she watched Tyler stroll toward her. Zipping her coat all the way up to her chin, she tried to pretend she wasn't as cold as she was. Freezing or not, he made her feel like summertime—warm and easy, full of promise. She nodded, appreciating his good looks as he neared. To give her time to "dress" he'd excused himself and gone to the corner store, and now he was returning with something sweet that was making her mouth water. And it wasn't whatever he was carrying in that paper bag either, her mind told her. She smiled while her eyebrows danced, then licked her lips. She wanted to kiss him. Badly. She could feel herself begin to pucker, and he wasn't even near her. "So whaddya got?" she asked to stop her kisser from kissing.

"This," he answered, saying something else, but she didn't know what. She couldn't hear him because she was too focused on his lips. Cherry. She bet they tasted like cherries. "So . . . ?"

Breezy crinkled her brows and shrugged her shoulders. "I'm sorry. Something was in my ear," she lied, hopping off the porch. "What's that again?" She reached for the bag and accidentally touched her hand against his.

"Hot chocolate." He handed her a sleeved cup and they walked down the street.

"Mmm," she moaned as if hot chocolate was the best thing she'd ever tasted, but the truth was, she hated it. She'd drink it though. Enjoy it because he bought it for her and she was sure he had the softest hands she'd ever felt on an athlete, but couldn't be one hundred percent sure. Great, she thought. Now she wanted to kiss him and hold his hand. It was going to be a long day, she just knew it. "So where are we going? To your mom's?"

Tyler laughed, grabbed her free hand, and rounded the corner.

Warmth flooded her and she blushed a little. He did have the softest hands she'd ever felt on a boy.

"This is okay, right?" he asked, looking toward their intertwined fingers.

Breezy looked down at their hands, loving how theirs fit together so perfectly. Gently, she squeezed, tightening their connection. "It's cool." Tela was crazy if she thought she was going to keep her promise and not push up on Tyler. She'd not only be a fool not to, but a no-feeling fool, and the tingle she felt in unspeakable places every time he was near, reassured her she felt everything. She didn't understand girls like Fats—the "good" girls. Breezy shrugged. She was good too. When she

THE BOY TRAP

was bad she was at her best—that's what her exes had told her. Besides, she wondered, admiring Tyler with a glance, who could stand to be around someone so fine and smart and NBA bound and not be affected? If she had her way, they'd have two-point-five children before he graduated college. And she wanted to start working on her family as soon as possible. Not only because she needed to secure her position, but because she really liked him, and wanted to prove it to him.

"So are you ready?" Tyler asked, pulling her out of her fairy-tale trance and stopping in front of a house.

Smoked barbecue met Breezy's nose and made her stomach growl. She rolled her eyes, laughed, and dropped her head until she was staring at her feet. "How embarrassing!"

Tyler laughed too. "I'll take that growl as a yes. C'mon." He pulled her up the driveway. "You're going to feel right at home. My family likes to eat!"

Breezy followed him through the gate and to the backyard. Two huge barbecue grills were on the patio next to the porch, smoking like it was the Fourth of July. Loud music and even louder laughter came from the house. She stopped in her tracks.

"You sure you want me here?" she asked, a little hesitant. She'd had boyfriends before, had been with them in crowded stadiums and gymnasiums, but never had they taken her home.

Tyler pulled on her hand. "C'mon, Gabrielle. Of course I want you here."

Her stomach roared like someone had pushed it past the point of pisstivity.

"And it seems like a part of you wants to be here, too." He opened the back door without knocking, and stepped inside, taking her with him.

Breezy smiled. Multiple brands of perfume sweetened the air, old men around her grand-daddy's age sat at the kitchen table playing cards, and laughter was everywhere. There wasn't one person in the house who didn't seem happy, and Breezy couldn't ever remember seeing a family so close outside of a television sitcom.

"What's your name, sugah?" an older gentle-man asked.

"Puddin' Tang," a mature woman answered him.

"Ask her again, she'll tell you the same," the other women sang out.

Breezy looked at Tyler for help. Either they were weird or she just didn't get it.

"They're just messing with you," Tyler said. "This is Gabrielle, everyone. My friend."

"Oh *friend*, hunh?" one man said.

The other men at the table laughed.

A pretty woman in a red hat with the same color fingernails took Breezy by the arm. "Come on, sugah," she said, leading her through a swing door that led to a huge family room with an eating area. "They're just messing with you because Tyler doesn't bring home friends too often. What's your name again?"

Breezy's lips were frozen into a smile. There were plenty of people in the family room too, seemingly all there to see her and look in her mouth when she spoke. That's how she felt because all eyes were on her. "Bree—I'm sorry. Gabrielle . . . ma'am," she threw in, knowing Tyler would appreciate her level of respect. He seemed like the overly respectful type, so she assumed she should be too.

"I'm Low Retta, Tyler's grandmother," the small, dainty woman said, cutting her name Loretta in two with her Southern accent. Everything about her said she was class. "Have a seat, sugah. I'll fix your plate. Tea with lemon?"

Suddenly, Tyler walked through the door into the room. He had a plate in one hand and a drink in the other, and he set them both on the table in the dining area. "Gabrielle, I brought you something." He nodded to the food, then went back the way he came.

Grandmother Low Retta just nodded and smiled. "Friend, indeed. Friend, indeed." She looked around the room at the other women, and raised her perfectly arched brows at a woman who looked like her twin, just years younger. She nodded. "*He* fixed *her* plate."

Breezy didn't know what to do. Should she sit and wait or stand and go eat? Her stomach was telling her to get her grub on. Her empty belly grumbled louder and clearer and she wanted to fall out and die, to disappear. *Oops.*

The woman stepped forward, walked in front of Breezy and extended her hand. She smiled. "Gabrielle?"

Breezy nodded and took the woman in with one glance. She had beautiful skin, pretty, natural, full thick hair, and the same café au lait skin as Tyler. *His mother.* Had to be. She stood and shook his mother's hand. "Yes, ma'am." She laid it on thick. "Nice to meet you." Her stomach rumbled again, and Breezy rolled her eyes playfully.

"Ms. Scott," Tyler's mother introduced herself. "And you're hungry. You'll fit in great around here." She led Breezy to the table.

"Same thing I said," Tyler agreed, walking back in and setting down his plate on the table.

Breezy sat down in front of her plate, in the seat next to his. She wanted to dig in, get barbecue sauce all over her face, and eat until she had to unfasten her pants, but she needed to impress him and make her future in-laws know she fit into the family.

"Gabrielle, eat up. Don't act shy around my mother!" Tyler teased. He moved his body close to hers and pecked her on the cheek.

Her eyebrows shot up. So Tyler was into PDAs? Cool. Her exes had never been down with public displays of affection, so Tyler was surprising her on all fronts. She glanced at him and wondered how many more surprises he'd give her, and what it'd take to make him give her the ultimate one.

Under the table, she reached over and patted his knee while she watched him through her peripheral vision. He ate as if nothing was unusual. Her hand climbed his leg closer to his thigh, and she squeezed again. He picked up his lemonade. She went farther still, and tightened her grip.

"Umph," he choked and jumped, gave her a sideways, hard-to-read glance.

His expression told her just what she needed to know. Tyler Scott, college-bound genius and NBA shoo-in was playing hard to get. Breezy licked her lips. It was only a matter of time before she got what she wanted. And she was certain she could get him by the night of the dance. She knew she couldn't ask him, he always had to be the man.

"So, Tyler tells us you two are going to a dance?" His mother made her night.

7

The Dance (still December)

Pish. Ssst. Pish. Ssst. Breezy's bustdowns slid across the floor and slapped against the soles of her feet as she walked across the linoleum tile. She'd worn her own trusty-dustys to the nail salon because she hated the cheap disposable ones they issued free of charge. Plus, hers were cuter, and Tyler had said he'd probably stop by. She climbed the elevated seat above the whirlpool bowl, kicked off her trustys and let them thump to the floor while her feet relaxed in the water. The pedicurist tended to her feet, and she wiggled her toes. "Sex on the Beach, that's my color," she said to Lady.

Lady poked out her cherry-glossed lips and wiggled her head. "Well, all right for Sex on the Beach! Maybe it'll rub off."

Tela sat up in the salon chair on the other side

of Breezy, staring at the bottle of polish Breezy held. "Sex on the Beach, my ras! You would've done better wearing closed-toe shoes, like me. That way you could've skipped the pedi altogether and saved yourself the nail polish hype—that color is champagne. No matter how they dress it up. I'm sure Tyler would agree . . . if he was here!"

"Dang, Tela," Breezy and Lady sang in unison.

"You're a dream killer." She closed her eyes, enjoying the attention her feet were being paid.

"Satan . . . oop! Oop!" Lady's words caught. "Speaking of Beelzebub." She pointed toward the entrance.

Breezy opened her eyes and gulped. *Not today*.

"Jay mutha-lovin' Sean!" Heavy eyelids batted with each syllable as Tela shook her head in disgust. "We need like a serious United Nations of all religions prayer group to save you from him, Breezy."

"He's still über fine."

"I know, Lady. Ultra cute."

Tela crossed her arms over her large chest. "Mmm-hmm. He's make-ya-drop-it-like-it's-hot gorgeous—then he drops you like you're hot. Hunh, Breezy? What'cha ras know 'bout that?"

"Shuddup!" Breezy cut her eyes. "You don't have to be so cold."

Tela nodded. "I'm just reminding. . . . That's all."

Jay-Sean strolled toward the pedicure bowls

with a fresh pair of Ones on and a matching towel hanging out of his front pocket. The crisp white of his kicks and the rag said he was surrendering. He winked at Breezy and smiled. His dimples caved into his cheeks like miniature bowls when he licked his lower lip, and she knew he was willing to do more than give in. Walking straight to her, he bent forward and kissed her on the cheek. "Eeezzzzay!" He looked at Lady and Tela as if they'd just appeared. "Wassup?"

No one said a thing.

Right then and there, he began taking off his sneakers. He looked over his shoulder at Tela, first at her face, then at her feet. "If you're not getting your feet done, you mind if I sit there? I want to sit next to my girl."

Tela rolled her eyes.

"If you move over I'll give you a cookie," he said seriously, but in a lilting tone, as if she was a toddler or overweight.

Breezy nodded her approval.

Tela snarled at Jay-Sean, then moved.

Jay-Sean grabbed the nail polish bottle from Breezy's hands, admired it, then read the bottom label as he settled himself in his seat. He rested his feet on the sides of the bowl waiting for a pedicurist. He turned to Breezy. "Sex on the Beach? Oh . . . you doing it up big now. With who? That new dude who tried to fill my position? Ain't no other player like me. . . . You and the entire population of Lakeview knows that."

Breezy batted her eyelashes slow and heavy like Tela, then looked away. She wanted to laugh, call Jay-Sean out on his obvious jealousy, but she didn't want to do it right now. She wanted him to hang himself on his own. "Who would you be referring to?"

Lady leaned in closer, obvious with her eavesdropping. She rested her chin in her elbow and raised her brows. "Yes, who?"

Jay-Sean cut her a look. "You know . . . pretty boy."

Tela kicked her leg over and touched Jay-Sean's. She grinned. "You mean the one who doesn't go around offering girls things that aren't good for them. The same nice guy who can run *and* bounce the ball at the same time, unlike traitors who leave Lakeview for more shine time?"

Jay-Sean flipped Tela the bird. "Remember, if you don't make nice, Fats, no cookies!"

"Wrong sista," Lady jumped in, taking up for Tela. "I'm the thick one, remember. And if you're not BSing, I'll take the cookies you keep offering."

"So, Jay-Sean . . . how's your girlfriend? The one we met?" Breezy cut in.

Jay-Sean looked around, then down at his feet. "You know I was gonna call you a few times—"

"Gabrielle? You picked out your polish without me?"

Breezy looked to her right, smiling. She hadn't seen or heard him come in. She looked at Tela and Lady. Both of their chins were dropped, so she knew he'd surprised them too. Quickly, she glanced at a stunned Jay-Sean, and was sure Tyler had caught everyone off guard. "Oh, I picked out a color. . . ." she began, then trailed off.

Jay-Sean held up the bottle of Sex on the Beach.

Tyler held up a bottle of a different color. "I think you'll like mine better, Gabrielle. Trust me."

"Word?" Jay-Sean said. "Mine suited her just fine. She never complained. Right, Easy?"

Tyler looked from Jay-Sean to Breezy. "Well, beautiful?"

Breezy gulped. She was so caught up that she'd become stuck on stupid, and couldn't speak. Her words were lodged in her throat, but her choice was easy. Tyler was the man for her. "That's a nice color," she said to Tyler. "Sorry, Jay-Sean. I think I'm going to rock with Tyler on this one."

Jay-Sean hopped out of the spa seat and stepped back into his shoes. "Good to try new things, Easy. But when you're really ready to rock—again—call me. You know how we do it, Breezy . . ." He walked away, then turned over his shoulder. ". . . Eeezzzzay," he called out like an ROTC sound-off from the door.

Her head was on his chest as he rocked her body ever so slightly. Breezy smiled, thinking about the wonderful night she was having. Tyler had picked her up in his mother's car, treated her to dinner, and showed her off at the dance like she was a star. She closed her eyes when he kissed her on the forehead, and was glad that she'd cho-

sen him over Jay-Sean.

"You like me, Tyler?" Breezy asked, hoping he'd fall into her trap tonight. Her mother was away again, and her father thought she was staying over at Lady's, and Lady's parents thought she was having a sleepover at Tela's.

Tyler stopped and stepped away from her. He looked down and smiled. "You a'ight," he teased.

"No, seriously, Tyler. I want to know if you *like me* like me? As more than a friend."

Tyler grabbed Breezy by the hand and led her off the dance floor. "Maybe it's time to go. You think?" He winked.

Warmth ran through her veins, and she was sure. Tyler was ready. "Let me go say good-bye to my girls. Cool?" she asked while walking away. She needed Lady's key and quick. She could see Tyler nod as she sped toward Lady.

"Awww'right. Sex on the Beach," Lady sang out, holding a cup of something that made her slur.

"Remember, I didn't get that color. And I know you're not drinking liquor, are you?"

Lady shimmered in a blinding silver dress. "I know you're not saying my sin is worse than yours. Yours is premedicated!"

Tela jumped between them. She wore a purple dress and looked like royalty. "Premeditated! You mean premeditated," she hissed at Lady. She turned to Breezy. "Benadryl with a soda chaser.

That's what she's been drinking. I told her not to have a carbonated drink with the medication, the bubbles make it kick in too fast."

"So . . ." Lady squeaked, then dipped her hand in her bag. She pulled out something and pressed it into Breezy's hand. "Here you go. The bottle of, and I quote, 'punch' "—she moved her middle and index fingers in an up and down motion like rabbit ears—"is under my bed."

Tela shot Breezy a look. "So you're gonna take advantage of him. Doesn't he get a say?"

Breezy snaked her neck, then looked at Lady like she could kill her. "Fats, you get me sick. I don't know what punch Lady's talking about." She opened her hand, showing the key. "She just gave me this so we can get into her crib." Breezy turned her attention to Lady. "You be careful with that Benadryl. I'll see you later?"

Lady nodded. "Yes indeedy, slick and Breezy. Don't do nothing I wouldn't do."

Breezy flashed a smile at Lady. "There's nothing you wouldn't do." She turned to Tela and stuck out her tongue. "Lighten up. I'm going to find, claim, and train, then tame my man."

"Call me Fats one more time, Gabrielle, and it'll be your ras! Treat me like I respect myself— and yourself too!"

8

_____

The After-Party

Music blared from somewhere as they walked toward the apartment building. Breezy bopped
her head to the heavy bass, familiar with the track.
She stepped over loose trash that littered the
front sidewalk as they made their way inside. She
paused, looked at Tyler, and bounced her head
some more to the rhythm. The song was old-
school hip-hop, something she'd been waking up
to for years thanks to her parents.

"Oww," she sang out, "that's my jam! What you
know about that, Ty—" she began, then closed
her mouth. Stinky smoke rushed them when they
entered the building. She cringed and held her
breath. She just didn't get it. Lady lived in a nice
apartment complex, but vandals weren't really
picky, especially when it was cold outside. Every-

one wanted to be in the heat, she guessed, relaxing a little when Tyler grabbed her hand.

"What floor?" he asked, pulling her through the hallway.

Breezy stopped in front of a door. "Right here." She reached inside her purse and pulled out the key. "Come on," she instructed, letting them into the apartment.

Tyler walked up behind her, and pushed the front door closed. "You sure this is okay, Gabrielle?"

Breezy nodded and kicked off her shoes. She slinked out of her coat and tossed it on a chair. "It's cool. Don't worry," she assured him, helping him out of his wool peacoat. "You know it's too cold outside for this little jacket."

Tyler tittered. "It's warmer than you think." He walked toward the living room sofa and looked at the photographs on the wall. "Is there anything in here to drink, Gabrielle? Coming out of the cold into this heat is a bit . . ." He cleared his throat.

Her eyes beamed. Getting him something to drink was exactly what her plan called for. She thought it'd be harder than this, but Tyler was making it easier than she'd expected. "Have a seat," she said, and headed toward the back of the apartment where the bedrooms were. She looked over her shoulder, saw Tyler getting comfortable, and was happy that he didn't know one part of the house from the next. When she was sure she was out of his sight, she moved with purpose, picking up speed. Lady's room was the last bedroom in the house and it felt as if she couldn't get there fast enough.

"There," she said, walking in and clicking on the light. Quickly she dropped to her knees and removed a paper bag from under the bed. She pulled out its contents. Triple X Ginseng, the juice of kings. "A powerful all-natural prescription. Manufactured in Kingston, Jamaica," she whispered, reading the juice's description. She threw her arms in the air, careful not to drop the bottle, and did a silent dance. Tonight was going to be the night, she just knew it. "One second, Tyler," she yelled out while she exited the room. She was in the kitchen before she knew it. She had snatched two glasses from the cabinet and ice out of the refrigerator. She poured them both a drink of real fruit juice and the ginseng potion.

"I thought you forgot about me," he said as she walked toward him.

Breezy looked at him and wondered how he could ever think such a thing. Yes, she knew he was only playing, but he was so fine that she couldn't even imagine forgetting about him in a nightmare. "Puhlease," she said, handing him his glass and sitting next to him. Their thighs touched.

Tyler lifted the glass to his lips and guzzled it down. His Adam's apple elevated and dropped with each gulp. Breezy watched in amazement, getting warm all over from excitement. As much as she wanted him, she hated to resort to this to get him. But he left her no choice. She moaned, just thinking about them being intimate made her happy. She knew how long it took to set the trap for Jay-Sean; she wondered how long it would take for Tyler.

"What are you over there moaning and smiling about?" Tyler asked.

She froze. *Oops.* "Didn't mean for you to hear that. I was just feeling out loud," she flirted.

"Feeling out loud? Oh . . . kay." He looked at her as if he were trying to look through her.

It must be kicking in.

"Gabrielle, I don't mean to be greedy, but is there any more left?" He raised his glass. "The juice?"

"Sure, baby. Tell you what, go to the last door at the end of that hall, and I'll bring it to you. Lady's mom should be getting here any minute, and I don't want to be all posted up on her sofa like we pay rent," she lied with a smile and a point of the finger. She took his glass from him, got up, and zoomed to the kitchen.

Tyler was splayed out on Lady's bed watching television when Breezy walked in the door with two more drinks. She turned off the lights and quietly set down her juice on the dresser. She tip-toed over to the full-sized canopy and eased onto the mattress next to him, careful not to spill his beverage.

"Here, Tyler," she said. She handed him the drink and picked up Lady's remote control. When

Tyler began to empty his glass, she turned the television to a satellite music station, and Trey Songz's magical voice filled the air, singing about somebody's neighbors knowing his name.

Tyler looked at her through glazed eyes.

Yes. He wants it too. She puckered her lips and blew him a kiss.

He pushed his glass toward her, stared, and nodded when she took it from him.

"I'll just sit this here," she said, setting it down on the nightstand. She grabbed his hand. "And I'll just put this here." She put his hand on her thigh.

His eyes were locked on to hers. Poor thing couldn't even blink.

Breezy bent forward, grabbed the sides of his face and pressed her lips against his. She had to have him, and imagined they were more in love than anyone who ever lived. "So . . . we're to-gether, right?" she whispered in his ear.

He moaned, "Mmm-mmm."

"And you want me just like I want you?" She planted soft kisses along his cheek and ran her hand over his waves. She closed her eyes and said a quick prayer of thanks. Yes, indeedy. Tyler was making this much easier than she had imagined.

"Mmm-mmm."

"You love me, Tyler?"

"Mmm-mmm."

Breezy would've cried if she had a second, but she didn't. Not now. Now she had to focus on the trap—getting him to give it up to her. She knew

THE BOY TRAP

without a doubt that if she could get him to go there—sex—there was no turning back. She'd have him on lock. Prom. College (for him). Baby. NBA. She'd get it all, and she'd stick with him through it.

"I love you too, Tyler," she whispered in his ear, pulling her long dress up just past her knees and climbing on top of him.

He moaned again, then started grinding under her.

Breezy almost screamed out, she was so happy. She didn't think the juice would kick in so fast, and had hoped he'd be a little more hands-on, but she'd take what she could get. *Oh!* An idea swooshed through her mind that she'd never considered. *Maybe he's a virgin.* That would explain a lot. He was nervous, she told herself. *Just nervous.* That's why he wasn't completely taking over like she thought he would. And that's why he'd turned her down when she was almost naked, lying across her bed. "I'm sorry, Tyler. This is your first time, hunh?" she asked, holding her breath and praying he'd answer yes. Because if she was his first, she'd definitely be able to trap him up quick, fast, and in a heck of a hurry.

"Mmm-mmm."

Yes! "It's okay, baby," she said, reaching under her and pulling at his clothes. "I'll walk you through it."

"Mmm-mmm."

"Was that a mmm-hmm or un-unh-no?" Breezy paused, asking.

"Mmm. Mmm-mmm-mmm!" Tyler moaned louder and his body began to buck.

"Mmm-hmm, yeah. That's what I'm talking about!" Breezy urged, trying to kiss him.

His head turned back and forth, slamming against the pillow. He began to convulse.

"Oh God!" Breezy yelled, jumping off of him and rushing to turn on the light. "Are you having an attack?!" She snatched her cell phone off the dresser.

Tyler's eyes rolled, but he was conscious. "Mmm. Mal. Gee."

Breezy walked up to the bed. "What!"

"Mmm-mal-a-gee," he said, repeating the same thing over and over.

She stood over him with her hands on her hips, not sure of what to do. "911?" she questioned, then dialed Lady. "We've got a problem!" she yelled into the phone. "Something's wrong with Tyler!" She pressed END and disconnected the call. Tyler was still mumbling. She leaned in and listened to him again as he continued to repeat himself. "Oh. *Allergy?* Are you saying allergy?"

Tyler managed to nod his head.

Breezy snapped her finger and ran to the bathroom. If Lady didn't have anything else, she had some Benadryl. Opening the medicine cabinet, she immediately spotted three big bottles of allergy medicine. She grabbed the first one she put her hands on, did an about-face and hustled back to the bedroom, twisting the cap open on her way. "Here." She handed it to Tyler.

He guzzled it down faster than he had the juice.

For minutes the world stopped. She watched his chest rise and fall, slow at first, then it quickened. He inhaled, looked at her, then shook his head.

"Are you out of your mind, Gabrielle?" he yelled, pushing himself up.

Breezy flinched. She'd never seen him angry before.

"What are you jumping for? I'm not going to put my hands on you. Real men don't hurt females," he said, walking up to her. "And males, females, whoever, don't touch someone else without their consent. What did you give me, Gabrielle? What kind of juice was that?"

She was two inches tall and shrinking quick. That's how he made her feel—inadequate and disrespectful. She excused herself, speed-walked to the kitchen and got the bottle of juice. She returned to the room and handed it to him.

"Ginseng? Are you freekin kidding me? I'm allergic to ginseng! That's why I can only drink soda and water and, sometimes, one-hundred-percent fruit juice. I told you that. I thought I did . . . the day we ate pizza and supposedly learned each other."

Breezy wanted to climb into her shell, but realized she didn't have one. "Sorry . . ."

Tyler's brows drew together, and he looked at her strange. He began to walk out the door. She reached out to stop him, but he snatched away and walked to the living room. "Do you realize that you were going to commit a crime, Gabrielle?"

Breezy sucked her teeth, disliking his bashing. She wasn't committing a crime, and they both knew it. "No, I wasn't. It's only juice—feel-good juice, but, still, just juice. I should know. . . . I drank some too. It had me all warm and tingly, so how was I supposed to know you weren't affected the same?" *It worked with Jay-Sean and me, me and Dez, even with Lady and her dudes*, she wanted to say.

He picked up his peacoat from the chair. "It is a crime, Gabrielle. Your intention made it a crime. You were going to *drug* me, or so you think, to get what you want. Tell me that's not wrong," he yelled, walking to the door. He turned the knob and opened it. "One more thing—ginseng does *not* make you horny! Maybe some guy tricked you into believing that and took advantage of you, but the truth is if it affected you in any way, it was all in your head. You wanted whatever feeling you had." He walked out and slammed the door.

Breezy ran to the back room and picked up her cell. She called Lady again. "Come quick . . . I

need you. Tyler just walked out."

Music blared through the phone, and it sounded as if a million hands were passing it and someone was covering the mic. Finally, a voice met her ears. It wasn't Lady's.

"Eeezzzzay . . . so, Lady tells me you're alone. Can I come through?" Jay-Sean asked.

Breezy looked at the ginseng and wondered if she should let it go to waste.

9

January

Breezy picked up her phone for the third time in ten minutes, and actually touched one of the keys with her acrylic tip before changing her mind. She was tempted to call Tyler, but didn't want to seem like she was playing herself. It'd been over two weeks since *the incident*, and he'd managed to shake her off his trail. She couldn't find him anywhere. He didn't answer his phone, was never home when she stopped by, and was off work for winter break. She looked at her cell, shook her head, and tried to understand what the big deal was. All she'd been trying to do was solidify their relationship, and make them both happy, and now he was punishing her for it. She'd believed he was just as attracted to her as she to him, so she didn't see what the problem was with indulging.

Her phone rang and she stared at the screen. Jay-Sean's name scrolled across the caller ID with a DO NOT ANSWER behind it. He'd come to Lady's house the other week just when she was on her way out the door. She'd been tempted to stay and play with him, but she was thankful she hadn't been so stupid. She knew that she was just something for him to use now—a fill-in when his main girl wasn't around and a target to get back at Tyler for out balling him on the court, with stats and scouts. When Tyler began to be highlighted on television, the light on Jay-Sean's ego began to dim. And she refused to be his pawn to make him feel brighter.

Setting the phone on the nightstand, she saw herself in her full-length mirror. She looked horrible. Yellow bleach-stained tights were painted on her legs under a gray and red oversized shirt, and a multicolored scarf was wrapped around her head, only to be outshone by the wire-rim prescription glasses no one knew she needed. She stuck out her tongue at herself, and guessed her yucky getup was a side effect of the math she'd been studying. She walked over to her closet to find a solution to her hideous outfit. Tonight some of the players from the basketball team were having a back-to-school get-together, and she'd heard through her personal grapevine, Lady, that Tyler would be there. So not only did she have to be present, she had to be drop-dead-fiyah-fly. Drake's ringtone sung from her nightstand, pulling Breezy away from her thoughts and closet.

She looked at her caller ID, and relaxed when she didn't see Jay-Sean's name on the screen. "Easy Breezy, beautiful."

"Run for cover, girl! I got that fast-track info—expedited. He will definitely be making an appearance."

Breezy raised her brows and looked around the room like *Who is she talking to?* then said, "I know that already, Lady. You told me last night. . . ." She twisted her expression. "Did you accidentally take too much Benadryl again?"

A loud breath blew through the phone. She guessed that was Lady's I-hate-when-you-ask-me-stupid-questions exhale. Everybody had one, she believed. "Oh . . . kay for that. It's January, I don't take Benadryl in January . . . well, not unless I'm out of my other allergy meds. You know what? Never mind. I'm calling to tell you to wear the best thing you've never had in your closet."

Hunh? Breezy walked back to her closet, rummaged through her clothes for confirmation. She nodded. "Lady, I don't know what you're talking about. Are you suggesting I have no hot clothes? 'Cause if you are"—she snaked her neck—"you'd be right. I don't have clothes. I have wardrobe. Everything in my closet is on."

There was a loud pause.

"You there, Lady?" Breezy had her hand on her hip. She wanted an answer. Now. "Are you trying to say I don't know how to dress? You must not remember who my daddy is."

Lady laughed. "Breezy, stoppit. I know who your daddy is . . . and I also know Tyler isn't coming to the get-together alone. We need to shop quick. Wrap you up in something he hasn't seen before."

Breezy's eyebrows shot to the ceiling and her jaw dropped south. It took her a second to collect herself, close her mouth, and gulp back her feelings of embarrassment and anger. She raked her glance across the room and took in the books and papers fanned across her bed. Proof that she'd been studying like crazy since *the incident* to impress him and, hopefully, win him back. He'd told her he was attracted to smart, pretty girls, and that's what she'd been trying to become to earn her NBA-and-a-baby dream. So he'd already replaced her?

"You hear me, Breezy?" It was Lady's turn to make sure she wasn't the only one on the line.

Breezy nodded, but she couldn't speak. It was only January, a few months after meeting Tyler, and she was already being replaced. She didn't get it. She hadn't slept with him yet, so what was the problem?

"Oh, *hell*o no!" She stomped her foot. "Not this time." She wasn't doing this again. First Dez, then Jay-Sean—there was no way Tyler was going to shake her too. It seemed like every boy she really liked and had planned Breezy-and-blank-sitting-in-the-tree for left her for someone else. Not this time, she decided.

"Not I, said the cat!" She looked at her phone as if she didn't remember having it; then she calmed a little. "Lady, I'll get back with you. Tonight or something. I'm not revamping my *clothes* to get him." She turned and looked at the books again, the paperback things she'd been borderline allergic to and now had actually started to find interest in. "I've been working on my *mind*."

She hung up, stepped into her orange slicker boots, grabbed her purse and keys, and snatched her seventies multicolor patchwork jacket her father had given her. She stormed out of the house forgetting she was rocking the yellow bleach-stained tights, dual-colored oversized shirt, colorful scarf, and glasses.

She was huffing up Tyler's block before she knew it. When he'd first given her his address months ago it seemed like he only lived a hop and a skip away. Even the last two times, when she'd popped up at his house hoping to catch him so they could talk, it seemed closer, but then, she had hopped out of cabs. When she shoved one foot in front of the other and felt the burn in her thighs, she knew she'd been wrong about the distance. Either that or she'd just been walking too fast.

She stopped in front of his house, and almost turned away. But she'd come too far to go back now. Besides, she told herself, she was Breezy.

She didn't back down from anything. Leaning her body right, she looked up the driveway and saw his mother's car. Relief relaxed her a little. At least this wouldn't be a wasted trip like the last two. The other times she'd come over no one was home, and she'd left without answers. If Tyler wasn't here, at least she could ask his mother his whereabouts.

The front door opened before she could climb the steps. Breezy gulped. She hadn't thought this through. She knew she was coming to confront him, find out his problem and how and why he'd replaced her so easily, but she wasn't prepared to face him. Not so soon. She wanted to at least gather herself before she knocked, but it was too late. He stood in the doorway, glaring at her as if she was the most disgusting thing he'd ever encountered.

She took her time lifting up her orange slicker boots and walking up the steps. It took her even longer to make it to the closed screen door. Already feeling defeated, she put her hands in her pockets and her heart behind a shield, preparing for the worst.

"Um. Hi."

Tyler nodded, and pushed open the screen door.

"I can come in?"

He just stared at her.

"Fair. I just came by to see how you could throw our friendship or whatever we had away. I liked you. Really liked you, but I guess it wasn't mutual. But we were still friends," came out in one breath. She blinked, trying to dry her eyes. "I know I made a mistake—went too far, but I said I was sorry. And I was, am. All I've been doing for weeks is studying. Studying and trying to get in touch with you. Then I hear you're bringing some other girl to the get-together tonight. . . ." she rambled, tearing up and shaking her head. "How could you? Really? So you were just going to show up with a girl on your arm at *my* school? I mean, it's your school too . . . but I'm the head cheerleader, so when it comes to girls attending our functions, *it's* mine."

Tyler broke his stare and a slight smile lifted the corners of his mouth. "So you've been studying, Gabrielle?"

Was he serious? she wondered. Here she'd stood out in the cold, been straight with him, had even blinked back tears, and that was all he could do, ask if she'd been studying? Tyler didn't need to say anything, he'd told her everything she needed to know with his actions. She gave him the shoulder shrug, then turned to leave.

He stepped out and grabbed her by her sleeve. "Where are you going? Come in," he said, pulling her inside the warmth of the house. He closed the door behind her, and stared at her face. "So when did you start wearing glasses?"

Now she was going to pass out. For real. Never mind saving face, she was going to hold her breath until she blacked out. *Oh gawd*. She looked down slowly and saw her pants and boots. She imagined he thought her outfit looked like a bag of Skittles had exploded in his house. This coming-over-to-make-up thing wasn't working. It couldn't have been worse.

He reached out, touched her head. "Gabrielle, I never pictured you wearing a scarf to bed. I guess I thought your braids fell perfectly every time you woke up."

Breezy fell back against the door for support. Just when she thought it couldn't get any worse, he made it so. She decided to take an interest in her boots. The more she focused on her slickers, the less she had to look at him. "I gotta go."

Tyler lifted her chin. "Look at me. You don't have to go, and you don't have to be embarrassed. I like you like this—thrown together. As stuck-up and full of yourself as you are, you coming to find me like this"—he looked her up and down—"tells me that you really care about me. You do, hunh?"

Breezy nodded.

"All right. I'll give you one last try, Gabrielle. We can be friends, and see where it goes. But no games and sex traps. Okay?"

Breezy's lips spread into a smile and she began to cross her fingers behind her back, then stopped. She wasn't lying about the trap, but she'd make him want her. She couldn't help it; she just loved him so much she wanted to keep him for life.

10

March

Gray. His bedspread was gray. Bluish-gray with hints of black and oatmeal, Breezy noticed as she lay across it with a book in front of her. Not in a million years would she have imagined that she'd be in Tyler's room, let alone on his bed with him next to her. Pushing her glasses farther up her nose, she bit on the eraser part of her pencil, leaving dents in the ribbed metal. Giving him a sideways glance, she admired him. He was fine. *Super-duper fine.* She inhaled his scent, still looking at him. He smelled good too. That solidified it for her. He was definitely the man with the plan who was blow-your-mind sexy. It was too bad she couldn't have him. Yet.

She'd been trying to crack Tyler harder than America was trying to unlock Leonardo da Vinci's code, and she swore her mission was harder. Still, she stayed on track to pull him in, and began to specialize in all the things Tyler liked. She stayed home instead of hanging out, chose attending class over skipping, and had swapped out selectively vision-impaired cuteness (purposely not wearing glasses to look cute) for funky wire rims that emphasized a different beauty in her. She'd even lost the weight of her extension braids and wore her hair more natural. And she was almost there, she could feel it. By graduation, Tyler would be hers, mind and body.

She turned toward him, admiring him head-on. They were undefeated. The basketball team had a winning streak, and so did she and Tyler. They'd done everything together. He tightened his skills and began focusing on which schools he wanted to attend, and Breezy tackled her schoolwork and filled out some college applications. She never sent them off, but she did at least complete them.

"I think we're good together," he said, startling her out of her trance.

She blinked. "I *know* we're good together. Catch up," she said, elbowing him. She really wanted to kiss him. She wanted to put her lips on his, hold his über-fine face in her hands and pull him to her, but she wouldn't dare try. Breezy had given him her word, no sexual advances and no sex traps. She wanted to keep him, so she had to find a way to make him think it was his idea.

Tyler closed his book and turned on his side. He removed her glasses and swiped her hair out of her eyes. Breezy blinked slow, feeling the seriousness of the situation. *Please God, let him kiss me.* It had been almost three months since *the incident*, and she'd earned at least that—a simple kiss, if not more. She shook her head, tripping at wanting him so badly and the fact that usually boys pressed girls for their goods, not the other way around.

"You're beautiful, Gabrielle."

She closed her eyes, took in "beautiful" and smiled. Ever since he'd told her that beauty was much more than being pretty, she'd waited on him to call her beautiful, and it was more special this time than when she was crying.

"Thank you . . ." She turned on her side and stared in his eyes. "So what makes me beautiful?" she asked, knowing it couldn't be the tears or her vulnerability like last time.

Her whole body warmed when he touched her breast with his finger; then she looked down and realized he wasn't being fresh, he was pointing to her heart. "This," he said, poking her chest again. "And this," he pointed out, touching her temple. "Your heart and your brain is what makes you beautiful. It sometimes only takes one, your heart or your brain, but you have both. You're double beautiful."

Breezy laughed. "So I guess that makes me doubly hot!" she teased, poking out her lips.

He pecked her lips with his, and nodded. "Yes, Gabrielle. You're doubly hot."

Her heart swelled and refused to deflate. Her eyes bucked and her breathing changed or stopped or something; she couldn't be sure because she was shocked that he kissed her. "Did you just kiss me?" she asked, unable to help herself.

Tyler nodded. "Mmm-hmm."

"Is that an mmm-hmm or an mmm-mmm. One means yes, the other means you're having an allergic reaction. I just want to make sure you're not allergic to my lips. That wouldn't be a good look."

He laughed. Looked her right in her eyes and laughed, and Breezy relaxed a little. If they were at the point of laughing about the night of the dance and his having an allergic reaction, they were going to be okay.

"Speaking of reactions . . . what would be your reaction to me asking you to go to the prom?"

She bit her bottom lip to keep from smiling. "Ask and see."

Tyler got up and slid off the bed. Breezy sat up, watching him. He walked in front of her and got down on one knee. Reaching up, he took her hand. "Gabrielle, yes, no, or maybe so?"

Breezy playfully pushed him back. "You're crazy. That's a will-you-be-my-girlfriend question."

"Why would I ask my girlfriend to be my girlfriend?" he asked with a straight face.

Breezy looked at him, waiting for him to laugh or smile or something, but he didn't. "You're serious. Girlfriend?"

Tyler doubled over in laughter, then caught his cool. "Yes, I'm serious. What do you think we've been doing all this time?"

"But you didn't ask me. I just thought we were friends." *And I was trying to get back in good with you so you wouldn't shake me.*

Tyler pecked her on the lips again. "Well . . . Gabrielle, since I have to ask you to be my girl-friend . . . will you? Yes, no, or maybe so?"

Breezy leaned in and gave him a genuine, fully grown kiss. She pulled back and looked him in the eyes. "Yes, I'll be your girlfriend—"

Tyler pecked her lips again, cutting her off. "You mean you'll *continue* to be my girlfriend . . ."

". . . if you let me pick our prom colors."

Breezy cradled books in one arm, and pushed her glasses up the bridge of her nose with her free hand. She closed her locker, looked at the clock at the end of the hall, and rushed down the hallway. She had math and didn't want to be late. Her grade had already risen almost two letters, and she was going for a B. She smirked, walking past the hanger-outers in the hallway, remembering when she used to be one of them and didn't have a plight in life either. Well, besides snagging a future NBA player. She tsked and felt sorry for them. At least she had a plan now. She wasn't going to snag and bag just any NBA player. She was going to snatch up Tyler.

"Where you rushing to?" Tela popped up out of

nowhere, pulling Breezy from her thoughts. Her messenger bag banged against her hip as she rushed to keep in step with Breezy.

Breezy sped down the hall, not slowing. "Class. Where else?"

Tela tilted her head, snatched Breezy by the arm. She stepped in front of her when she stopped, and reached toward her face. She tried to take off her glasses. "I think you forgot something. Did you know you had on these—"

Breezy reared back her head. "I wore these on purpose. They make me look studious."

"Studious?" Tela blinked her heavy lashes and a confused look washed over her face. "Okay, Gabrielle Newton, we need to talk. Immediately."

Breezy flinched. She hated when Tela called her by her full name. When Tyler called her Gabrielle it was cute. But when it rolled out of Tela's mouth it was scary because it sounded too much like her mother, and it made Breezy feel like she was going to be put on punishment.

Tela pulled her down the hall and into the bathroom.

"Wait," Breezy protested. "I'm gonna be late for class."

Tela crossed her arms over her chest. "I never thought I'd say this, but shuddup about going to class. Okay? You're weirding me out. I can't take such a drastic change in such a short time. You go from lame and loser to fame and future—it's too much!"

Breezy laughed. "I know you're just playing about being lame, Tela. Better had've been. But it's cool. I'm just starting to like this math thing a little bit."

Tela leaned in close, smelling Breezy's breath. "You been drinking? Or just frontin'? First class, then you're calling me by my real name. . . . I know Lady has you thinking—"

"Lady has her thinking what? That we're going to be the hottest girls to step foot up in the prom?" Lady asked, walking up to them and popping her gum. "My aunt's seamstress said come see her Friday so she can start designing your dresses."

Breezy and Tela looked at her. "Where did you come from?" they asked in unison.

Lady rolled her eyes. "Oh, I forgot. . . . *Both* of you go to class now. This is my hangout. I don't have a class this period. And Lady probably has her thinking what?" she parroted Tela.

"Probably that I can trap Tyler . . . that's what she's always talking about, us trapping boys with our . . . oops!" She snapped her finger. "So you hang out in the bathroom, Lady? That's lame," Breezy said.

Lady pointed her index finger and snaked her neck, looking at both of them like they were crazy. "Well, duh. *Yeah*. I hang out here until I can sneak out the exit two doors down. You know I gotta wait until the adults clear the halls. I'm not trying to get suspended months before graduation."

Tela's lashes rose slowly. "So . . . you're graduating?" she deadpanned.

Lady pushed up her sweater sleeves like she was ready to box. "See, Fats, that's your problem. You don't know when to quit. Why would you say some dumb ish like that? I'm not stupid. Of course I'm graduating—*and* going to college! How 'bout that, Fats?"

A huge smile spread across Tela's face. She reached out, pushed Lady's hands down to her sides and hugged her. "That's great, Lady. Dead serious. Me too."

Breezy looked at her two best friends and was happy for them. "Well aw-righty for you two! Do that college thing, and I'll be rooting for you from whichever state drafts hubby."

Tela wore a quizzical look when she glanced at Breezy. She hunched her shoulders. "Are you sure?"

Breezy nodded and waved away Tela's question. There was no way she was going to anybody's college. She had a hard enough time going to high school. She just wasn't with waking up early in the morning and doing the school thing for four more years for a little piece of paper and bragging rights.

Lady looked numb and disappointed.

"What's your problem, Lady?"

"I know we talked about the NBA and babies and money, but I guess I just thought that that's all we were doing—talking. And after you've been going hard studying . . ." She shook her head. "Don't tell me all of this is to trap Tyler."

Breezy looked at her watch. She was ten min- utes late. "Oh, I guess since both of you've decided to go to college, now you think alike, because you sure are talking alike. 'Trap Tyler'? I'm not trapping anybody, I'm just securing my future. College is not for everyone. I was born to be rich and important. I don't have to go to school for that—I can get both of those from marrying a baller."

Tela walked out the bathroom, and Lady just nodded.

11

End of April

Breezy adjusted her custom dress, then tightened the straps on her shoes. She unfolded
herself like she was putting on a production and
did a hard spin, then slowed it down, swaying her
hips to make the fabric billow.

"Well, what'cha think?" she asked Tela and Lady
as they stood by a car, idled in front of the venue.
Other prom-goers bypassed them and made their
way inside. The girls were dressed to the nines,
happy to be there, and most of the boys looked
like they were there only to match the girls' gowns
like the perfect bag or pair of shoes. Breezy's glance
shot Tyler's way, and she smiled. His suit was the
perfect fit to her dress because they'd both literally been cut from the same cloth. Well, at least his
vest had been.

Lady, forever in red, stuck her asthma inhaler

in her mouth, pressed two quick pumps, and inhaled. She paused and closed her eyes for a second while the medicine kicked in. Suddenly, her lids shot open, and her cell rang. She flipped open her phone. "I think your dress is hot, Breezy. Fiyah!" she said on the exhale, and then turned her attention to whoever was calling. "I'm right here. . . ."

Tela walked up to Breezy, and straightened the side of her dress. "I see why you kept it a surprise. I think it's beautiful. You're beautiful, Gabrielle. Canary yellow looks good on you." She seesawed her heavy lashes, looking like a mother hen. "Now move your ras. Me and Lady got boys to link up with inside, and Tyler's over there waiting for you. He looks like he's suffering. Better hurry before your father interrogates him some more and decides to show up." She tilted her head toward the patch of grass where Tyler stood with Breezy's cell stuck to the side of his head like it was glued on, while her father talked to him.

"You think I look good enough tonight to bag Tyler? Gotta lay this trap on him if I want to keep him and go to the NBA with Mr. NBA . . . 'cause there will absolutely be no college for me. So I would hope he finally gives in—it *is* prom night. And he can't stay a virgin forever. Don't know why he be girlin' and has me acting like a hard-pressed dude. . . ."

Tela crinkled her nose. "A virgin? You sure?

That's not a bad thing. . . . At least you know he can't give you something you can't get rid of . . . like a disease."

Lady just nodded. "You're good, Breezy. How can he say no to you *tonight*?" she asked, covering the mouthpiece of her phone.

"He's threatening him," Breezy mumbled, referring to her father. She walked away from her girls and toward Tyler. She grabbed the phone, said they had to go, and promised her father she'd be safe and yada, yada, yada, then hung up. She laced her arm through Tyler's. "Come on, Mr. NBA. We've got a prom to turn out and pictures to take."

Semi-hot music blared, overdressed teens mingled. Breezy and Tyler posed for their pictures, circulated the room, and did their job: they were the ultimate super couple, wearing their jock and cheerleader pride on their arms like honor. Then they left and made their way to the real party. The one in the hotel suite around the corner that Lady's cousin, Dynamo, was more than pleased to rent for them—for triple the room price, of course. One third went to the hotel, the other two thirds laced Dynamo's pockets, and they had to buy him some chicken wings and barbecue corn chips!

Breezy kissed Tyler on the cheek, then watched him walk over to say what's up to his teammates and a few friends. When she was sure he was settled, she looked around for Tela and Lady, and noticed refreshments were being served in the corner of the room. She stared at Tyler until he looked at her, held up her hand like it was wrapped around a cup. "Thirsty?" she mouthed.

Tyler nodded and winked.

Breezy headed over to the crowded table, waiting her turn. Her mouth became drier by the second. She looked back over her shoulder, saw Tyler was engaged in conversation with his boys. She looked the other way, scanning the crowd for Tela and Lady.

A giant collided with her. "Sorry, Breezy," one of Tyler's teammates, whom she recognized as one of the Echo Boys who ran with Doo-Wop, apologized, looking down at her.

Staring up at his face, she tried to remember his name, but couldn't. He was a waste of almost seven feet, riding the bench more than hooping. "No problem."

"You been waiting here long?"

Breezy nodded.

Echo Boy grinned like a Cheshire cat, reached through and over the people crowding the table, and handed Breezy a drink.

"Thanks, but I don't drink . . . alcohol."

"Well, you're good then. Neither do I. It's just punch. I assure you."

Breezy scrunched her shoulders and painted a *please* look on her face.

"Let me guess, you're getting a drink for my boy Tyler, too? It's cool, that's my teammate. If it weren't for him we wouldn't have swept everyone off the list. Now just about all of us are college bound . . . full ride. Even me," he said, diving back in and coming up with another drink. "I was just going over there. I'll take it to him if you want. I think your girls are over there somewhere," he offered, nodding his head toward the back of the suite.

"Thanks!" Breezy said, gulping down the stale fruit juice. She looked toward Tyler, and saw Echo Boy bring him the drink. Tyler nodded at Breezy, then winked again. *Yep, it's gonna be on tonight!* She was sure.

She walked the circumference of the three-room suite toward the back, and her heart caught in her throat. She was sure that was Jay-Sean standing with his back to her, just feet away, but wasn't sure. He wasn't dating anyone at their school, at least not that she was aware of.

"You better get your ras outta here, Doo-Wop!" Tela's voice blared over the music and pulled Breezy's attention. Sure enough, there was Tela's money-green dress standing out in a sea of pastels and blacks.

Breezy high-stepped across the room in her high-heeled strappy sandals, speeding over to the direction of Tela's voice. "S'cuse. S'cuse. Move! Thank you." She made her way through the crowd, forcing herself through and around some cliques that refused to budge or separate. Lady's dress snagged her attention next; then she almost threw up in her mouth. Right in front of everyone's eyes, whether they knew it or not, Doo-Wop's hand rested in the middle of Lady's lower back. *They're together?* "Yuck . . ." *How can she stand his sewer breath?*

"Excuse me. You okay, Fats . . . I mean, Tela?" She walked up to the group, which was thicker than she'd believed. There had to be at least ten people gathered, she guessed.

Lady's head drooped and she stared at the floor. Doo-Wop had a stupid cheese grin plastered on his face, his jaw still hanging to his chest.

"Well . . ."

Everyone was silent and they all looked constipated, like they were holding something painful. Breezy looked from face to face, then stopped. There he was, the real Mr. Dynamo. Jay-Sean. He wore all black, and his suit hung on him like he was a coat hanger. Her ex was draped in deliciousness, and it was bothering her. She turned her eyes to Tela, waiting for an answer.

Tela nodded. She laced her arm through Breezy's. "Let's go."

"Tela, wait . . ." Lady's voice trailed off when Tela shot her a nasty, gut-wrenching look, and almost growled.

Breezy reared back her head, twisted her face

until it looked as if she smelled something stinking. "What's up with that? What's going on?"

Jay-Sean walked up in front of her. He took her free hand, raised it, and put it up to his mouth. He turned it over and licked her palm. "I hear your man's not giving it to you."

Breezy immediately raked her eyes to Lady and lunged a little.

"Nah, Gabrielle," Tela said, still holding her arm.

Jay-Sean was still holding her hand to his mouth, and planting little kisses up her arm, but Breezy didn't notice. She was too busy trying to telepathically tell Lady to be woman enough to look up from the floor and into her eyes.

"So is it the truth?" Jay-Sean asked. "Your man . . . excuse me. Your *boy* won't give you what you've been fiending for?"

"Look at me, Lady!" Breezy urged, snatching her arm from Jay-Sean. "Look at me!" she yelled.

The room started to quiet.

"Why . . . ?" she screamed.

The room silenced.

Lady shook her head.

Doo-Wop laughed, sipped his drink, then sipped some more.

The hotel suite came to life again.

"Don't be asking my girl why, yo? She didn't tell . . . *you* did, Easy Breezy."

Breezy almost broke her neck, turning her full attention on Doo-Wop. She snatched her shoulder forward, trying to get Tela to let go of her shoulder. "What do you mean *your girl* and *I did*, Doo-Wop?"

Lady started crying.

"First you called my boy Jay-Sean and had him meet you at my girl's house the night after the dance, then tonight . . . Tela, Lady . . ." he sang, laughing and trying to make his voice sound feminine. *"Tyler be girlin'! Acting like he can stay a virgin forever. You think I look good enough to make him hit me off tonight? Gotta lay this trap on him 'cause I want to go to the NBA with Mr. NBA. No college for me,"* Doo-Wop sang, almost getting her words correctly.

"Lady? Why did you tell him . . . ?"

Tela pulled her shoulder again.

Jay-Sean laughed. "Even had his drink spiked. Dang, Easy . . . I didn't know you was so hard up. You coulda just came home with me. I would've tore you out the frame . . . like old times. Well, not that old."

Her world was caving and she was lost. *Spiked drink?* "What the . . . spiked drink? What?" She was beginning to rage thinking about Echo Boy offering to get a drink for her and Tyler—a thing she'd always been warned about, taking drinks and food from strangers. Tela was still pulling on her shoulder. "Let me go!" She whipped her head around and felt herself die while still breathing.

"That true, Gabrielle?" Tyler said, his hand on her shoulder.

Doo-Wop was full-blown drunk. His mouth hung and his breath was rank, but no one seemed to care. Not with all the information he was giving. "Gabrielle . . ." he said, making a production out of hitting Jay-Sean, to get his attention. "The *new* Mr. NBA calls her Gabrielle. Tyler, man. Don't you know her name's Easy? Easy Breezy 'cause she's *easy* to hit . . . a basketball trick, right, Jay-Sean?"

12

—

May

The grass swiped across her flat ballerina shoes as she walked across the school grounds. He was there, just feet from her as she made her way over to him. She gulped, trying to swallow her fear, but her shame was in the way. Tyler hated her. She knew it. She'd done everything she could to speak to him, but he wouldn't hear her. She shrugged as if they were back at the hotel, because what else could she do? She couldn't deny anything. When he asked her if Jay-Sean had come to Lady's, all she could say was yes; then he'd silenced her before she could explain the rest. When he pressed her about applying to colleges, she couldn't answer in the positive because she hadn't applied to any and had no intention. All she wanted was to sleep with him, have a baby, and ride off his coattails to fame.

"Big mistake!" she whispered, correcting herself. She shook her head, and approached him, hoping he'd at least hear her out today. Quietly, she walked behind him and tapped him on his shoulder. "Excuse me?"

Tyler turned and his face changed from beaming to regret. He didn't say anything.

"I just wanted to talk to you before . . ."

He shook his head. "You don't have to explain anything to me, Gab . . . I'm sorry." He tilted his head and looked at her like she was the most disgusting thing he'd ever laid eyes on. "Breezy. Easy Breezy, right? Easy . . ."

Now it was her turn to shake her head. "No." She stuck out her hand, hoping he would take it. "I'm Gabrielle Newton, and I'm really sorry. I know you won't forgive me enough to be my boyfriend again . . . but it's okay. I just wanted you to know that I'm truly sorry . . . and I did not spike your drink. After the ginseng thing . . ." She shrugged. "Well, you know."

Tyler took her hand and shook it. "Nice to meet you, Gabrielle. I really wish I would've met you— the *real* you, and not some girl who goes by the name of Easy Breezy—when I first came here. I think we could've been great friends . . . but only friends. The whole sex and gold-digger thing doesn't really work for me. . . ."

Gabrielle nodded. "I know."

"And you're worth way more than what's between your legs. You know that, right? Your worth is in your heart and brain—that's all I was trying to get you to see."

She nodded again. Whether he believed her or not, she got it. She understood, and no Jay-Seans or Dezs of the world were going to make her forget again. "Well, good luck with the NBA. I heard they want you as soon as they can have you. What's the rule now, one year of college?"

Tyler laughed. "Not with my mother. The rule is finish college!" He shrugged. "I want to work on something besides basketball. I want an MBA and to start my own business. Basketball, even the pros, doesn't last forever."

Gabrielle thought about her dad, and knew Tyler was right.

He reached out and straightened her cap. "I guess we better get ready. We're graduating today, Gabrielle." He gave her her name back.

She smiled and nodded, then went to go find Tela and Lady. Lady may've slipped up and forgot to cover the mouthpiece of her phone the night of the prom, accidentally allowing Doo-Wop to hear Gabrielle, but she was still her girl. If Lady wanted to be with a mouth-breather whose breath could end the world if he sneezed too hard, that was on her. She turned, and called out to Tyler. "Hey, Mr. NBA! Don't forget about me when you make it to the playoffs! Work on your inside shot, and know I'll be somewhere cheering you on and sideline coaching from the stands or in front of the TV. Who knows, possibly even grad school."

"Gabrielle!" Tela yelled from across the grounds, and Gabrielle swore she could see her blinking. "Over here!"

"Yes, Bree—I'm sorry, *Gabrielle*. We're over here!" Lady said, emphasizing Gabrielle, then stuck her asthma pump in her mouth.

Gabrielle walked up to her friends and wrapped them in a bear hug, her arms unable to hold them both. "We're doing it, girls! Yessir."

Lady held up her hand. "Wait! I got something to tell you."

Tela's eyelashes lifted and dropped, seeming an inch longer and a pound heavier. "Tell it."

Lady shook her head. "I couldn't do it no more. I swear I couldn't."

Gabrielle drew her eyebrows together. She didn't like the look Lady wore, and she was becoming concerned. "What? You couldn't do *what*?"

Lady held her hand to her chest, inhaled and exhaled until her chest literally rose and fell where everyone could see. "After that trickery and backhanded stuff . . . Doo-Wop's breath!"

All three doubled over in laughter.

Gabrielle lay across her bed with a book in front of her and a pencil in her mouth. Old-school hip-hop blared and made her bob her head. She tried to shake off the rhythm and get her concentration back. She'd been in deep thought, she realized when she looked at the ribbed metal rim that housed the eraser and saw she'd left numerous teeth indentations. "Aw-righty," she said, getting up and going to close her door. She lay back down.

Her door burst open. "What's the matter? You don't like my music anymore," her mom asked.

Gabrielle smiled. "Nevva that! I'm an old-school head."

"I know that's right."

"Mom, can I ask you a question?"

Her mother walked in the room and sat on the bed. "This sounds serious. You okay."

"Why did you and dad break up? I mean you had it all. A big house, professional ball-playing husband, beautiful daughter, money out the yinyang. You had everything."

Her mother played in Gabrielle's hair. "I guess it seems that way, but I didn't have *me*, Gabrielle. Your dad and I were high school sweethearts, and we were being too grown too soon, and we had you—beautiful you. So we did the right thing. We got married. Your dad went to college and the NBA, and I went to . . . nowhere, and I wanted so badly to go to college. . . . That's why that was the first thing I did after the divorce. I wanted to be an individual. A woman with power." Her mother bent down, and kissed her on the forehead. "You know where power begins, right?" She touched her temple with her index finger. "Here and in your heart."

Gabrielle nodded. "Yes, I know. Power and beauty begin there. Thanks, Mom."

She watched as her mother got off of her bed, then left out of her bedroom. Seconds later music met her ears. "I'm sorry," her mother yelled, still not turning down the music. "Is that too loud for you, Gabrielle?"

"No, ma'am," she answered, getting off the bed and walking to her door. Minutes ago, her mother was disturbing her, but now she'd set the tone. Her mom had not been some groupie NBA wife like she'd once believed. And if her mom was too good for it, then so was she. Everything that had happened in her life in the last few months pointed out that her worth was off the chain. She didn't need a baby to begin life. She didn't need a super-duper, über-fine, extra-rich NBA player (preferably a starting player) for a husband, though she'd still opt for some money and looks, but not for a long, long time.

She locked her door, then went to her closet and rifled around until she found a stack of notebooks. She removed one, then dived across her bed. She rearranged the books she'd been reading earlier and slid them on the bottom. She nodded. Now she knew what she needed and wanted.

Opening the notebook, she wrote down the date, then began:

Dear Break-up-to-Make-up Diary,
Today, I'm applying to college . . .

Don't miss Kelli London's debut novel,

Boyfriend Season,

coming in August 2011 from Dafina Books.

Turn the page for an excerpt from
Boyfriend Season . . .

"This school can kiss my entire *asssk* me no questions and I'll tell you no lies!" Santana Jackson mumbled as loudly and inaudibly as she could, breezing past Beekman, the summer school principal. She wanted him to hear her, just not be able to *prove* what she'd said. Cursing in the Atlanta public school system was forbidden— a major violation she thought ridiculous and refused to be penalized for. She didn't do detention, and had no plans of starting today. She had more important things on her agenda, like shopping and meeting her boyfriend, Pharaoh. Besides, if her mother didn't care what she said, who were the teachers to question what escaped her lips? Plus, being on lockdown in a classroom was raggedy with a capital R. But rappers, thugs, and corner boys—hustlers around her way who made things happen by connecting the dots, they were a different story. Foul-mouthing gave them street credibility, made them more appealing. Delicious. Who didn't want a dude who was saucy, could feed your pockets, stomach, and mind, and spat "shawty" through platinum and diamond grills covering their teeth?

Pausing in the middle of the hallway, Santana turned and mean-mugged Beekman, who'd quietly fallen in step behind her. Wondering how long he'd been following her, she wore her disapproval like a mask, silently dared him to question her being in the almost desolate hallway during class time, then shrugged her shoulders in a what's-up-what'chu-wanna-do gesture. When she wasn't met with opposition, she mouthed "I didn't think so" to the principal's lack of action, then hoisted her book bag over her bra strap, swooped her index and middle fingers through her belt loops, and hiked up her too-tight jeans to cover her butt that Rashad, her neighbor, referred to as an onion. An apple. A badonka-donk that served as a compliment in the hood. Then she exhaled, realizing she'd been holding her breath and that she had an audience. A smile tugged at the corners of her mouth when she noticed two boys staring. They were admiring what was beneath the denim separating their eyes from her juiciness, so she got her sway on, moved her hips like a pendulum while their eyes followed the switch of her hips. She was fly and knew it.

"A'ight, Santana!" they greeted with a head nod.

"Yep." Santana threw up the deuces, a closed peace sign, and kept it moving. Yes, they knew her name, but so did just about everyone else in the school. She was Santana Jackson. Pharaoh's girl. And they were just fans.

Her phone vibrated in her purse as she pushed her weight against the door, exiting with a bang. It was almost one o'clock, close to their predetermined meeting time. Her feet lightened with each step as her shoes connected with the concrete beneath them. As always, she couldn't wait to see Pharaoh. Not only was he her dude, he was *the* man. His name rang bells, and his hood power preceded him. There wasn't anything that Pharaoh couldn't do—except Santana. She wasn't going to give in to him or be like one of the floozies who dropped their panties to guys because they were fly. She knew better and vowed to heed her mom's example: If you give a guy what he wants, he has nothing to stick around for, but if you give him just a smidge of what he wants, he'll stay for the rest.

" 'Bout time! I was just calling you. I thought I was gonna havta come up in there and jailbreak you," Meka Blackman, Santana's best friend, said, snapping closed her cell and leaning next to the door.

"I know, right? I tried to leave faster, but Principal Beekman was parading around like he running something, so I had to walk the halls for a minute," Santana answered as they left the grounds and turned the corner.

"So we scared of principals now?" Meka teased.

Santana shrugged and walked up to the passenger door of the "borrowed" pickup Meka was driving. "I ain't scared of nothing. But I'm not doing detention for nobody . . . especially not two days before summer school lets out. I'm not trying to risk doing a repeat. Ya heard?" Meka clicked open the locks with the car's alarm remote. Santana stepped up into the cab of the truck and asked, "How long you got this one?"

Meka stuck a key in the ignition, turned, and winked. Throwing the gear in drive, she brick-footed the accelerator. "Until whoever's-this-is pays my brother. He must owe him big time 'cause the rims alone on this gotta be at least ten stacks. Don't worry, I'll get you to your man on time. First we got biz to handle, though." The truck blew down the street on the ten-thousand-dollar rims, zooming faster than any speed limit in the country, blasting music. "You ready?"

Santana held on tight. "Turn that up! Is that Trill's new song, 'Talum'bout'? We gotta cop us tickets to his next concert."

"Yeah . . ." Meka agreed, nodding her head to the song, the title a southern twist on the words *talking about*, then mouthed the gutter lyrics. "That's that ish." She turned up the radio. "Okay, enough. We got biz to handle." She muted the speakers when the hottest teen rapper's song went off.

"And I'm ready too. You got my silencer?" Santana asked, referring to her boosting bag, the one they'd lined with foil and magnets and other things that prevented stores' security detectors from sounding off when they exited the store with stolen goods.

Meka smiled and took a sharp corner on Peachtree, headed toward Lenox Mall. "Nope. I didn't bring your silencer, sis . . ."

Santana scowled.

". . . I brought you two. Your old one and a *new* one. Check in the back. Now fix your face! Over there looking like someone pissed in your cereal," Meka said, then laughed.

Santana joined her, then reached into the backseat of the truck and retrieved a big brown, recycled shopping bag. She was proud of her friend. "Even thieves are going green!" she teased.

"Ha-ha. I made some extras this morning 'cause I got orders to fill," Meka continued while Santana pulled a new tote from the brown bag.

"This the new *Gucci*? Jungle tote? The two-thousand-dollar jammie?" Santana's jaw fell in her lap while she admired the bag.

"Yep. *And* it's a silencer. Merry Christmas in the summertime. Don't say I ain't never give you nothing," Meka rattled. "ADT, Brinks . . . Atlanta Police Department, they can all kick rocks. Ain't no alarms gonna ring with all the stuff I lined our bags with!" She laughed and whipped into Lenox's parking lot.

Santana hugged Meka as soon as they hopped out of the truck.

Meka shrugged. "Don't be too happy. It's a knock-off, but no one can tell. Not even the employees that work at the store. Trust me. I returned one knock-off last week."

The M.A.C. counter was calling her name when they entered the mall and walked past Macy's, but she knew she didn't have time to stop. She was there to "shop" for a few items, maybe pick up some new J's, and then meet Pharaoh out front. He was due to pick her up in less than one hour.

"Where you wanna hit first?" Meka asked, smoothing out her sundress, then her extra-short hair that was styled to perfection as usual. "You need a new Louis, right?"

Santana walked beside her, shouldering her dressed-up boosting bag and rocking her black and purple high-heeled Air Jordan 8s. There wasn't a soul who could tell her she wasn't a showstopper. Pausing in front of a store window, she checked her reflection. Fingering the top of her hair that was expertly spiked in a Mohawk, she turned sideways and admired how her graduated length cascaded down her back. *Even if I didn't grow this, no one can tell me my hair isn't fire.* "I do, but wrong mall. Louis is in Phipps Plaza across the street. You always forget."

"Right. Phipps. Too expensive and too much security for me. I'm not trying to get locked up again," she answered, capping her lip gloss and putting it in her purse, signaling she was done and ready. "You're cute. Come on," Meka said, interrupting Santana's beauty session.

"I know. You too."

Meka grabbed her wrist, then pushed Santana's hair from her face. "What? When did you get these?" she asked, fingering Santana's earrings. "These are ultra hot!"

Santana blushed. "Pharaoh had them made for me. If you look carefully, you can see P's in the design," she squealed, proud of her man.

"That's what's up. He's claiming his woman! Now it's time to get to work." Meka tilted her head; then they both nodded. If they were going to boost, they decided long ago that they'd better do it dressed to the hilt so they would be inconspicuous. Being raggedy would make security hawk them.

A crowd of dusty teenage boys walked past them and headed back toward the entrance of Macy's. Run-down sneakers, last season's clothes, jeans sagging too low, and voices talking too loud, they were definitely targets for mall and department store security. They were also the distraction Santana and Meka needed to keep them under the radar.

"Guess Macy's it is," Santana said.

Silencer bag filled to capacity, Santana exited the third store they'd hit and headed toward the escalator. Her adrenaline rushed, her heart raced, and she was sure she was shaking. It took every ounce of willpower she had not to turn around to look to see if they were being followed. She was nervous. Just nervous, she told herself.

"Dang. I can't believe we didn't hit Macy's. We got the other two good, though. Hunh? Where we going now?" Meka said.

"We need to go upstairs. That's where the J's are," she said, leading Meka through the mall, past the Starbucks, and finally to the escalator. "One of us needs to buy something. I'm gonna cop the J's for Pharaoh." She stepped on the ascending stairs, then turned around so she could check their surroundings while she was speaking to Meka. "We're good. Nobody's thinking about us."

Meka's expression was twisted. "Why you buying Pharaoh something? Shouldn't it be the other way 'round?" she asked, hopping off and following Santana.

Santana laughed, then entered the store. "Girl, nah. He always buys me stuff. A pair of J's ain't nothing. Plus, for what I'll get in return . . . it's a good investment. Anyway, I want my man to look good."

"Don't keep him looking too good. You know them floosies at your school be after him. Especially Nae."

Santana sickened. She couldn't stand Nae, her ex-best friend who'd gone after Pharaoh at a party. "Meka, forget it. Don't even bring it up. He don't want Nae. How could he . . . after this?" Santana turned slowly, showing off her ample curves and tiny waist, then swung her weave while strutting over to the men's sneaker section. She grabbed the new J's and Ones off the display, then asked a salesperson to bring her a size-twelve pair of each.

"Hmmm. Don't ever say what ya man won't do. K?" Meka said, following Santana to the counter.

Santana turned on her three-inch-heel Jordans. "Why Meka? Is that a warning or a hint? You know something? Talk to your girl, Meka!" she said, peeling off a few big bills, paying for the sneakers.

Meka eyed the money.

"Courtesy of Pharaoh." Santana took the bags from the salesperson.

Meka walked out, shrugging. "I'm just saying, Santana. Don't ever be so sure. K? Nae may not be fire like you, but just like ya man, she gives courtesies too. Maybe not cash, but her courtesies rhyme with cash."

"And I'll kick her in hers if she tries me again," Santana pointed out as they exited the mall. "There's Pharaoh's car over there. I'll call you later, Meka." She blew her best friend air kisses, then sashayed toward her man. "'Aye, baby!" Santana waved and cheesed so hard she was sure her teeth would shatter. The wind swept her weave off her back and moved her closer to him.

Pharaoh played with the chew stick in his mouth, biting and turning and sucking on it as if it were sugarcane. He gave Santana a head nod, reached over and opened her door. "S'up, shawty? You lookin' kinda right in dem there jeans."

Shaking her head, she put her bags in the backseat and suppressed the melting feeling that swept through her every time he was near. Pharaoh had a way of appealing to her senses, starting with his street talk. Everything he said, no matter how simple, was beautiful to her because she loved his ghetto-fabulous country grammar. Sidling into the seat next to his, Santana leaned her weight to the left until her shoulder touched his, then wrapped her arms around him and met his lips with hers, giving him a sweet peck. They could've shared a seat and, still, she couldn't be close enough. "Thanks. You what's up. Where're we going?"

Pharaoh roared the Charger's engine, reared back his head, and spread his butter-soft lips into a sneaky smile, revealing a platinum and rose-gold grill. "Er'where, shawty. Ya know? If you still rollin'." He threw the gearshift in drive, released the brake, and accelerated until their heads indented the headrests like they were on a rollercoaster.

Santana powered down her window, letting the warm Atlanta air flow in and the blaring music out. She bopped her head, reached over and ran her palm over his arm, loving the way his skin felt on hers. It was intoxicating knowing how powerful her man was. *There's nothing he can't do.* With T.I. rapping in the background, Santana looked over and admired Pharaoh. Paper-bag brown, fresh low cut with natural waves, he had just the slightest under bite that made his chin jut forward, causing him to look hard all the time. She took her hand, rubbed it over the hair he was growing on his chin.

"What up? You don't like that, shawty?" He looked over, flashed a slight crooked-tooth smile that revealed his platinum lower teeth, then stopped the car at the red traffic light.

She blushed. "You know I do." She reached in the back, retrieved the bag with his fresh kicks in it, then handed it to him.

He accepted the bag, then looked in it. He opened it and pulled out the Nike box first. A smile surfaced followed by a low laugh. He nodded. "That's why I'm wit you, shawty. You a good girl and you know what it is. That's why I got a surprise for you too. Shii, you asked me where we going? Stick wit ya man, baby, and we going everywhere. Straight to the top, shawty. Straight to the top."